THE MAGIC
WE DO HERE

THE MAGIC
WE DO HERE

———•———

LAWRENCE RUDNER

HOUGHTON MIFFLIN COMPANY
BOSTON / 1988

ACKNOWLEDGMENTS

I want to thank John Sterling, my editor at Houghton
Mifflin, for his great help and faith in my work;
and my agent, Rhoda Weyr, who has never stopped
offering assurance and wise advice.
I would also like to thank some fine writers, artists,
and friends for their help: Rod Cockshutt, Angela
Davis-Gardner, Michael Grimwood, Sue Hall, John
Kessel, Kit Knowles, Tom Lisk, Ann Mann, Joe Mann,
Damienne Real, Leslie Real, and Lee Smith.
I am grateful to my family — Rudners, Greenbergs,
and Kershenbaums — for their love.
Finally, I owe more than I can ever say to my
children, Elizabeth and Joshua. This story was also
written for them.

Library of Congress Cataloging-in-Publication Data

Rudner, Lawrence Sheldon, date.
The magic we do here / Lawrence Rudner.
p.   cm.
ISBN 0-395-45034-9
I. Title.
PS3568.U333M34   1988   88-558
813′.54 — dc19   CIP

Printed in the United States of America

P 10 9 8 7 6 5 4 3 2 1

For Lauren,
who made everything possible

and

In memory of a beloved friend,
Joseph Kelly Sobkowski,
1946–1981

I know with certainty that a man's work is nothing but the long journey to recover, through the detours of art, the two or three simple images which first gained access to his heart.

— ALBERT CAMUS

I was surrounded by objects which had all of them changed. Something never before experienced had crept into the substance of reality.

— BORIS PASTERNAK

THE MAGIC
WE DO HERE

1

LET'S BEGIN with the map, shall we? If you find a map of Poland (not a current one, please, for the borders have changed) and spread it out on a table, you will see all the major cities that may or may not appear in our story: Warsaw, Lodz, Bialystok, Poznan, Krakow. Now, when you find Warsaw and the great river Vistula that passes through our rebuilt capital, run your finger along this thin blue line in a northwesterly direction until you meet the river Narew and the small town of Nowy Dwor, the birthplace, before the awful whirlwind, of the great artist Chaim Turkow. Here you may stop and ask: Why look back at such a time when the present is difficult enough? Who needs to be tossed backward into Gehenna? But we ask for your patience, since we know that our simple story can't possibly make you feel sad or lost. Here is why: We will begin with a miracle that took place in the town of Nowy Dwor (still in our old Poland), long before all of the Jews disappeared in a mist.

✦ ✦ ✦

On a very cold day in November of 1922, Moishe Turkow, a Jewish innkeeper, witnessed the birth of his fifth child in the large family bedroom of his hotel, which faced the Narew River. To be truthful, we shouldn't say that Moishe Turkow "witnessed" this birth, for he felt such activities should only be reported *to* the father *by* the midwife and the other women. Still, he did run back and forth between his wife Lena's room and his packed downstairs tavern, certain that, after four daughters, his fervent prayers for a son were about to be answered. "She's carrying very low," he told the Jews who crowded around him. "There can be no mistake this time!"

When the midwife, an old woman who came all the way from Kutno, sent Moishe Turkow's youngest daughter to fetch her father for the great announcement, Moishe was so nervous that he stumbled three times as he climbed the stairway. "Hear, O Israel," Moishe said to himself again and again, "give me a son to hold."

If the Jews of Nowy Dwor were still with us, they might tell us how they never heard anything as terrible as the screaming and deep moaning that soon echoed in the upstairs hallway. Curses in Yiddish, Polish, even Russian drew the frightened Jews from their beer and vodka to the stairway. "A pogrom!" one of the men shouted as he ran for the rear doorway. "Hide!" And when the Kutno midwife was chased from Lena Turkow's lying-in room, everyone was sure the frightened Jew was right: the old woman's smock was as red as a squashed poppy, and she still held the shiny metal forceps at her side when she began pleading for protection "from the madman who jumps at people like a Cossack."

There was no pogrom. There were no frenzied Ukrainians banging against the window with hammers and axes in Lena Turkow's room. "Tell us," the Jews shouted. "What is it?" As soon as the midwife was safely covered by the huge back of Nowy Dwor's best butcher, Mordcha Rostzat, she yelled just like a peasant. "It's only a daughter . . . a beautiful daughter!"

So it was. A daughter. The fifth child of Moishe and Lena Turkow, born, the midwife was quick to report, with no problems except those created by the father in front of his crying, sweaty wife and cringing children. This is what happened: When Moishe entered the room, he was even more certain than before that the tiny, red-faced baby his wife gave him was a boy. "He's here," Moishe yelled. "My Chaim! Look at him, Lena, already he comes to his father for his first lesson in being a good Jew. Chaim!" Before anyone could tell the joyous man that he was indeed now holding Manya Turkow, who had been on God's earth for ten or eleven minutes, Moishe Turkow gave his first lesson to the squirming, dark-haired infant. "The Talmud," Moishe beamed, "is the source of all wisdom, little son. It says —"

Moishe never finished his sentence. The baby cried. Lena cried. Four Turkow daughters covered their faces. Through her sobs, Lena forced out the words and then pulled the stained bedcover over her head. "It's not permitted," she cried, "that girls should study Talmud, Moishe."

The reports of Moishe Turkow's anger were vividly told in great detail by the Kutno midwife. First, "this wild man from Gehenna," as the woman was now calling Moishe, nearly dropped the newborn child; next, he staggered full-weight against the bed, dragging his wife's bedcovers with him to the floor; then he screamed (this is what the Jews in the tavern heard) that he was "cursed," deserted by God and the rabbi's solemn promises, little more than a despicable worm in the mud! And that's not all, either. For Moishe Turkow smashed two chairs and one expensive vanity mirror, and loudly threatened the Kutno midwife with his fists (he actually gave chase to the hapless woman, but, with the aid of Lena's aunt, she got through the door before he caught her; all the while she was flailing away at him with the forceps).

In all, it took Mordcha Rostzat and two other Jews fifteen minutes to pull Moishe Turkow, the best innkeeper in Nowy Dwor, from the room. The butcher threw a pillowcase over his friend's head and bound his arms with the leather strop he always carried to sharpen his knives. Someone sent for the rabbi, another for the town's apothecary. Moishe's rolling eyes immediately suggested to the rabbi that the innkeeper was in no mood to listen to the learned man's imploring voice. But when the apothecary nervously approached Moishe, the innkeeper opened his mouth and obligingly swallowed a mixture of sweet tea and laudanum. Moishe Turkow then slept for one day, tied to the bed he and his wife had inherited from her parents. He later told his friends how he remembered nothing at all about his rage. He also refused to speak to his wife or his daughters.

Just before the Chanukah celebration, Moishe decided to rejoin his family. Although his wife was still frightened for her tiny newborn daughter, she was comforted by her husband's surprising tenderness and affection on that first day of the holiday of lights when Moishe, who had not even looked at her or mentioned her name for one entire month, gave each of his daughters a package filled with honey-soaked biscuits, imported cashews from South America, and lovely silk scarves he'd ordered for the occasion from Warsaw. The Turkow girls — Rachel, Gitl, Sara, and Miriam — were ecstatic to have their father in such good spirits again; and little Manya, her lips working furiously to take in her mother's nipple, cooed and chirped when Moishe tenderly put a fur cap on her already-beautiful head. "It's from Warsaw, too," Moishe beamed. "The

smallest fur hat ever made by the firm of Zalman and Sons."
Lena got some chocolates and a new prayer book.

That night, the first time Moishe had slept with Lena since
the onset of her pregnancy, he whispered to his still-worried
wife that, as soon as she was able, they would try again. "I had
a vision," he said before he fell asleep. "And I know what I
have to do."

Lena awoke to find her husband dressing before dawn. "I've
said my morning prayers. You nurse the little one. I am going
to swim in the river." But when Lena reminded him it was now
December, near freezing, and that a swim in such cold water
meant certain fever and probable death, Moishe said he was
"prepared." Everyone who heard Lena's plaintive cries thought
the innkeeper had found his old madness again, especially the
Polish fisherman who poked holes in the ice-glazed section of
the Narew and watched Moishe jump (no wading, you understand; Moishe Turkow had no fear!) into the water. Every
day the same: morning prayers, the chilly swim between the
floes, a run back to the inn with his shirt off, and a breakfast of
groats fried in rich garlic butter.

We have to tell you this: Moishe Turkow had had a dream.
Maybe it was some residue from the apothecary's laudanum,
maybe not — but Moishe Turkow would tell anyone who
cared to listen about a voice that spoke to him after the birth of
Manya when he lay, tightly buckled to the bed, in a pool of his
own urine. "Make your body and spirit as one, Moishe
Turkow," the voice urged in melodious Yiddish, "and a son
shall be yours." "Every night I heard this same voice," Moishe
said. "Every night the same. Now, you see, I know what went
wrong before!"

Except for those days when Lena was impure, Moishe was

ferocious in his lovemaking, a young man again whose muscles gave Lena little rest. His supplications and devotions to the Holy One, Blessed be He, took on a new urgency. He memorized whole passages from difficult Talmudic commentaries to discuss with the rabbi, bought a new set of leather-bound prayer books, and donated satin-covered chairs to the synagogue (along with a new stove for the rabbi's drafty house). He arrived at the studyhouse before anyone else and, though he wasn't sure whether it was permitted, threw himself to the cold floor as a servant would to his master. "A son, a son," he muttered to himself between lines of prayer. "Give me a son to bring up as a Jew."

Four months after the birth of his fifth daughter, during the first warm spring day for the Jews of Nowy Dwor, Lena told her husband that, yes, she was pregnant again. Moishe kissed her, ran to embrace each of his daughters, who stood in the hallway (Lena had asked them to be there when she broke the news, "just in case"), and, for extra luck, swam to the far bank of the Narew. Hands grasping the river's mud, Moishe pulled himself from the chilly water and threw his hands toward the clear sky. He rolled over on the grass that was just beginning to turn a mottled green and rolled backward, howling, into the river. "I knew it!" Moishe Turkow yelled in Yiddish to the startled Polish peasant who watched the crazy Jew. "Blessings to God, I just knew it!"

To the other Jews in Nowy Dwor, Moishe Turkow became a possessed man. He prepared for the birth of his sixth child with all the care a skilled engineer devotes to the building of a great bridge — from the special food he demanded Lena be given four, sometimes five times a day ("Lots of green vegetables, raw eggs from thick shells, and the best brandy mixed with brown sugar") to the doubling of his daily quota of prayers and Talmud study. He opened his inn's larders to the scores of Jewish beggars who soon learned about the generosity to be found in Nowy Dwor, and, though Moishe Turkow never told the rabbi, he even gave the parish priest enough money to buy a cow for the joyful Easter season ahead. All in all, Moishe Turkow leaped through the months of his wife's pregnancy like a racehorse that knows the outcome of the contest before it has even begun.

Six hundred pages of Talmud later, Moishe calculated that Lena would give birth before the Holy Days in autumn. He sent out invitations to all the relatives he had throughout the province, begging them to be with him at the birth of his son. It was Moishe, by the way, who first used the word "miracle" to describe what was about to happen.

And no more hag-midwife, either. This time, Moishe sent for a real doctor from Warsaw, a Jewish practitioner who was only too happy to come to the backwater of Nowy Dwor when Moishe Turkow offered him a free room, the best food and wine he could consume for as many days as he chose to stay, and a handful of gold coins. "Stay with her, doctor," Moishe urged the soon-to-be-sated physician. "Don't let any of the women touch her. *A man should bring out a man.*"

"He will be a scholar," a deliriously joyful Moishe told his assembled family on the afternoon Lena's pains began to make her swollen belly heave and throb. "My Chaim will know the Holy Books so well that his name will be repeated throughout Poland. Rabbis from as far away as Vilna and Lublin will come to sit in my son's study to listen to the truth." That said, Moishe retreated to the studyhouse in his best holiday suit and waited with the rabbi for the great moment. "Hear, O Israel . . ."

One hour before twilight, while Moishe sipped tea in the

courtyard of the studyhouse, the Warsaw doctor dismissed the female retainers from Lena Turkow's room when the inn-keeper's wife closed her eyes and nodded that she was finally ready. Not more than five minutes later, the doctor, as he'd promised, raised the window of Lena Turkow's sixth lying-in room with his slippery hands and, though he thought it mad, heaved an empty wine bottle through the shutters to the cobbles below. Moishe celebrated the splendid crash by hugging the rabbi. "My sorrows have broken up like that bottle," he shouted as he ran to his newly painted inn, inviting along the way every Jew he met to come with him to view the miracle.

You can imagine what Moishe Turkow must have been feeling when he approached the open door of his wife's room! Four of his daughters were dancing in the hallway, distant cousins from Zyardow lovingly passed his wailing infant Manya from hand to eager hand, and Mordcha Rostzat swung around his head the leather razor strop that, not too long ago, had served to restrain his lifelong friend and fellow Jew, Moishe Turkow. It took the innkeeper a full ten minutes to push his way through the cheering celebrants. "Please, my friends, let me see my child," he begged.

Why should we keep you in suspense? On a silk sheet embroidered with his son's name in silver thread, Moishe Turkow, the most devout Jew and best swimmer in all of Nowy Dwor, first caught sight of his Chaim. The innkeeper's legs were like tubes of rubber, however, and he had to will his body to cover those last few paces to his son. Chaim Turkow, born into a world of such calculated joy for his future and his soul, his father, the Jews of Nowy Dwor, and the rabbis of Vilna and Lublin, was, without doubt, the most beautiful living being Moishe Turkow had seen in his thirty-eight years as a dutiful servant of the Holy One. Moishe cried, prayed aloud, kissed his wife, kissed the Warsaw doctor, and ran his fingers through the luxuriant golden hair of the squirming son who took up such a tiny space on the sky-blue silken sheet.

2

O F ALL PLACES, the miracle ended in the steam of the Jewish bathhouse in Nowy Dwor, three days before Moishe Turkow planned to show off his beautiful four-year-old son to a visiting rabbi from Bialystok.

You must, of course, understand that Chaim Turkow had, by his fourth year, become the pride of Nowy Dwor's small Jewish community. It's true. This blond-haired and blue-eyed child of Moishe and Lena Turkow — these features alone were a source of wonder to anyone who saw him — had already learned Hebrew in his second year, he could recite from memory lengthy Talmudic passages by the time his hair was cut after his third birthday, and, in a moment that caused the old rabbi to fall swooning into his velvet studyhouse chair, Chaim Turkow became the only four-year-old in the collective memory of the community to correct a boy ten years his senior on the correct pronunciation of an Aramaic verb.

"There's no doubt about it," the rabbi managed to say when he regained his composure. "We need to support this child's genius." So that very night, while Moishe Turkow watched his son fall asleep in the oversized feather bed, the rabbi wrote a long letter to the most respected yeshiva scholar in Bialystok. "Come and see this boy for yourself," he begged his former mentor. "He is what we have been waiting for!"

The return letter that arrived from Bialystok took ten days in transit to Nowy Dwor, but the news it contained took little more than ten minutes to spread throughout the community. "Most beloved and honored Rabbi Ayzik Fayvlovitsch will come to Nowy Dwor," the great man's secretary wrote.

"He's written fifty important commentaries, and his students carry his words in their hearts," the rabbi excitedly reported to Moishe Turkow and the other leading Jews. "In only three days, Moishe, your boy will meet the teacher of teachers!"

Moishe thanked the rabbi and, gurgling with emotion, asked Lena to bring Chaim to the inn's dining hall. "It's because of you that we will have a new star in heaven," he said, lifting the boy atop the marble counter next to the prize crystal from Slovakia. Natually, no one refused the offer of a free meal the innkeeper ordered to celebrate this latest part of the miracle.

And here is how it soon all ended in the steam. Moishe Turkow was just too excited and anxious to enjoy the sumptuous meal his wife offered to his company. He choked on the stuffed derma, the apple tarts gave him gas attacks, and Lena's special raisin bread made him dizzy with energy. There were, you see, too many details to worry about: a new suit for Chaim had to be ordered and made ready within two days; the boy would need time to practice a recitation for the rabbi's visit; every Jew who loved Torah would have to be invited and fed the best stews and wines; and, without doubt, Moishe Turkow would immediately begin, along with his obedient son, the cleansing ceremony in the bathhouse that was necessary, certain obscure texts noted, for bodily and spiritual comfort.

Hand in hand, Moishe Turkow and Chaim led a small procession of Jews to the communal bathhouse (renovated by Moishe only a year before). They sang like Hasids at a wedding, twirling and raising their arms as they walked along the alleyway. The Polish women who saw the Jews walking through the market square thought some new and mysterious edict had moved the Jews' sabbath up a few days, and when the happy men approached, the peasants' noisy chickens were held aloft, prices sent flying in all directions.

"Ten zloty for your best steam," Moishe ordered the hunch-backed bath attendant, who was none too pleased with these sudden arrivals at day's end. "And twenty more if you join us for your trouble!"

No one had ever seen the hunchback move so quickly. He raced to the pile of wood and loaded the copper furnace with his choicest hard birch pieces, furiously pounding the leather bellows with both feet while hanging on to a hook attached to the ceiling. The fire established, he filled several oaken buckets with filtered water, washed down the smooth floor, and prepared the softest white sheets and towels for these very important and wealthy Jews. Only then did he proudly beckon them to follow him into the earthly cloud he had created for their pleasure.

It's not that Moishe Turkow forgot about his son when he settled himself on the highest wooden plank next to the old rabbi and Mordcha Rostzat. It's just that Moishe was so busy talking to the others about the upcoming visit of such a distinguished guest that he didn't keep his eye on the little boy who knew so much Hebrew. Each one of the Jews who huddled next to him had a suggestion the innkeeper was obliged, out of respect, to listen to: this one wanted the great rabbi to offer a special sermon on Shabbos; another, squirming his way next to Moishe's ear, insisted on paying the rabbi a "magnificent stipend"; a third wondered if the rabbi would agree to discuss the current situation of Polish Jewry now that Marshal Pilsudski was in firm control in Warsaw and there were actually Jews sitting alongside Polish nobles in the Sejm. Even Nowy Dwor's own humble rabbi, wrapped in a soaking white sheet like a paper-covered doll, cleared away the billowing steam long enough to demand that he be allowed one hour of privacy with Rabbi Fayvlovitsch.

Finally, after enough haggling and compromising that would have put Solomon's court to shame, the rabbi's schedule was agreed upon by all parties, and Moishe Turkow was satisfied that he'd finally pleased every influential Jew in Nowy Dwor. Then the hunchback, who swung back and forth on the trapezelike swing that gave him full view of his shrouded customers, heard a diminutive cry that sounded from the high seat enjoyed by the innkeeper and his amazing son. Pulling himself toward the disturbing high-pitched squeaks, the little man waved his own towel to clear away enough steam to see Chaim Turkow upended like a small frog. The boy had fallen between the warped board and the wall, and his blond head was twisted to the side like a braided challah.

Moishe Turkow, unaware of anything except his own excitement, reached out for his son's back, but the only skin he felt was on the hard bump of the hunchback, who'd lowered himself to help the boy. Moishe yelled his son's name, a panicked cry that made the Jews who were with Moishe Turkow kick open the heavy bathhouse door so that the hunchback, now next to the boy, could get some fresh air to blow into the small mouth of Chaim Turkow.

In the few minutes that followed the rush of cold air into the inner bathing chamber and the first gulps of the hunchback's beer-and-garlic breath into his lungs, Chaim Turkow began his new life — for though he was soon breathing again and wore the calmest smile, he refused to, or couldn't, speak: not to his father, who stood over him shivering and crying in a wet sheet, nor to the rabbi, who leaned over and patted the wet strands of hair on his star's golden head. Moishe shook Chaim, threw cold water over his face. Nothing could erase the boy's benign smile or bring speech from the once-perfect throat.

In the coming weeks, everything was done for the only son of Moishe Turkow. The Jews of Nowy Dwor acted as if the Messiah himself had come to Poland with a terrible illness that required immediate attention. The Warsaw doctor was again summoned by phone, exotic medicines were given, letters were written to the medical academies throughout the country, compresses and salves were applied to every inch of Chaim's small body, prayers were offered.

The hunchback repeated the story a thousand times of how he made the hottest and best steam thirty zloty could buy, but not enough, he yelled back at his inquisitors, to hurt anyone at all. "So the boy got a bit scared. What could I have done? He fell off his seat and twisted his neck or something. A bump on the head doesn't mean the end of life. What could I have done?"

Moishe Turkow's daughters sat with their brother throughout the cold nights and sang his favorite lullabies in two languages. And still, the same smile, the same silence. Yet, thanks be to the Holy One, the boy took nourishment from his mother, sipping the broth she cooled with her breath, relieving himself in the water closet with no assistance from anyone, and showing, once the triangular red patch disappeared from his forehead, no outward signs of illness or impairment. "Give me an answer," Moishe Turkow shouted to any number of expensive physicians who marched up the inn's stairway to examine, poke, and prod the splendid-looking boy. "Tell me what I have done!"

When the tenth physician hired by Moishe came to examine Chaim, he, too, was baffled by the boy's "exotic behavior," though he did offer an explanation, translated into Yiddish — with difficulty — for the sake of Moishe and Lena Turkow. "A nervous convulsion of momentary hysteria," he said (at least these were the terms the young man remembered from the article he'd once read in an Austrian medical journal).

Moishe Turkow left his son's room before the doctor had finished speaking. He walked to the stairway where his wife and daughters stood, reported what the doctor had said — "A compulsion, Lena . . . the boy was taken by a 'mysteria' " — lowered his arms in frustration, and, before anyone could stop him, smashed his head again and again into the nearest carved banister post. Town gossip would later have it that the only doctor who earned his fee was the tenth one to visit the son of Moishe Turkow, the very one who eventually managed to close the open gash on the innkeeper's forehead with sixteen neatly sewn stitches.

✦   ✦   ✦

Moishe Turkow thought he was cursed. It's not that he didn't share in the prosperity that was evident in his filled rooms and much-praised dining hall. No, in fact, Moishe worked like a galley slave for the next few years to improve his business so he could reinvest all he earned in properties or factories that would fatten his daughters' dowries. And it's not that he ignored those lovely, olive-skinned girls, who, as everyone said, grew more intelligent and attractive by the day. It's just that there came a time when, after one of his typical fifteen-hour workdays, he would, with much sadness, have to pass by the room where his silent Chaim usually sat in an overstuffed chair, listening to his mother read or sing to him while he held a pencil or crayon over a blank sheet of paper. "Talk to him all the time," Moishe told his wife and daughters, without much faith in his own wisdom. "Just keep talking!"

This, you see, was Moishe's curse: to be forever reminded of how he, Moishe Turkow, misinterpreted the promise of future greatness God once planted in his dreams after Manya's birth. Mordcha Rostzat blamed Moishe's sadness on the laudanum that must have, the butcher claimed, "stayed hidden somewhere in Turkow's brain" when everyone thought the innkeeper was mad; Moishe believed something or Someone beyond the drug's limited abilities was responsible.

Of the countless doctors Moishe continued to bring to see his son, only one, a recent graduate of some Italian medical school, was finally brave enough to advise the innkeeper to place his son in an institution. "What good can you do for him," the well-dressed physician said after a cursory examination of the mute Chaim, "if you persist in dreaming he will regain his speech or senses? What will happen, Reb Turkow, when you are no longer here to care for him?" Moishe listened to the articulate practitioner until he heard the word "dream." Then, as he had already done so many times, he paid the exorbitant fee demanded by this honest and earnest man, helped him pack his leather bag, and openly confessed that he didn't believe in dreams or visions. "A curse is a curse, doctor, but maybe one of you will know a good trick to help the boy."

Despite Moishe Turkow's dark moods and somewhat diminished faith, he never allowed his son to be treated like an invalid or an idiot. He made it part of his daily ceremony to wake Chaim every morning so the boy could watch his father wrap the *tefillin* and pray. Then, before breakfast, they always spent a few silent moments together, sitting in the dining room of the inn or, in pleasant weather, on the front porch. They often held hands. Moishe Turkow, his wife Lena, and their four oldest daughters had, it seemed, finally accepted Chaim's fate and certain future.

But Manya, the fifth daughter of Moishe Turkow, now fourteen years old, disagreed: *she* didn't believe in fate, the doctors' predictions, or her father's pessimism. If her parents sighed and shook their heads whenever they spoke about Chaim, Manya smiled. If she overheard the Jews of Nowy Dwor gossip about her brother in the marketplace or in the synagogue ("Bad luck for Moishe Turkow," they would say. "It's a shame his fool can't go to the Holy Books," or, "How could those beautiful eyes be placed in such an empty head?"), Manya would run home, dash up the stairs to Chaim's room, and take out the thin silver box with the special colored chalks. "Come, Chaim," she'd say. "Let's make a new world."

A new world indeed! Colored chalks. A pad of heavy white sketch paper. Manya and Chaim sneaking out of the inn before anyone else heard them. Manya dressing her brother, promising him that no one would ever know they were gone and, as part of the trick, hiding Chaim's feather pillow beneath his bedcovers. "Sha, sha, my artist," she always said to him if he showed the slightest resistance to her, "today will be the day." Then, their feet wrapped in rags to muffle their steps, Manya and Chaim Turkow went, as they had done secretly for years, to the birch wood by the Narew River to draw stars, moons, and animals. For her special designs, Manya preferred the darker-colored chalks; Chaim always chose the yellows and reds.

All of this began when Manya first invited Chaim into her castle when she was five or six. Still too young to be accepted by her older sisters as a playmate, Manya decided to hide in the tall armoire in the corner of Chaim's room. "This is my castle," she said. "It will cost you one zloty to enter!" And even if Chaim came running over to her without the required coin, Manya would put her skinny finger over his mouth, swear him to secrecy, and spend hours playing with him in what then became *their* castle. With all the frenzied activity in Moishe Turkow's inn, no one ever noticed her absence or, what's more important, suspected she was teaching her little brother everything she was learning from Mrs. Rosenblum in the Jewish Primary School for Girls. In that small, confined space below her father's spare holiday suits, Manya taught Chaim to form Polish letters and words, to recognize where Poland was on the colored map in her geography book. When she had her first drawing lessons from Mrs. Blumenthal, she showed Chaim how to trace, then sketch, simple figures and designs. "Now your turn," she liked to say after she drew a three-dimensional box or a cylinder. Chaim followed every instruction, bettering her own drawings within minutes. Yet he never spoke or made any sound.

Soon, however, the armoire-castle became too confining for a growing teacher and pupil, especially since Manya was now dramatically reading to Chaim long passages from a book mistakenly sent to her father by his favorite bookseller in Warsaw. Moishe Turkow opened the package (he was expecting a new commentary on the Babylonian Talmud) and found instead a leather-bound Polish translation of Rudyard Kipling's short stories, a certain Englishman Moishe had never heard of. Of course, Moishe immediately threw the expensive book into the dustbin. But Manya found it (how could anyone, she thought, not want to keep a book with such beautiful illustrations of tigers, elephants, and brown boys with white towels wrapped around their heads!), read it through in two nights, and soon invited her brother into the wonderful jungles and exotic cities that Pan Kipling had invented, Manya told her brother, from the comfort of his warm country home in England.

Thus did teacher and pupil, actress and audience of one, make their way from the castle they'd outgrown to the birch wood they adopted as their private jungle. Manya read; her brother listened, and always, at every tale's end, clapped when she finished. But on one July afternoon not unlike the countless others they'd spent by the river, Chaim waited until his sister was well into her reading before he took his own set of chalks, quietly opened his sketchbook, and drew the most perfect picture of Manya Turkow astride a baby elephant. "Why aren't you paying attention?" she asked when she saw her brother's eyes fixed on his paper. "What are you doing?"

Chaim tore the paper from his sketchbook and stood upright on the low, flat stone that served as his favorite chair. He held the sketch in front of his face so that the elephant hid his eyes. Manya stopped reading and was so taken by the shaded lines forming her own likeness that she didn't hear the first sound that Chaim Turkow had made in over eight years. "Chaim! You've made me," she yelled.

Perhaps it was his sister's tone that made him try again. Or maybe it was the way Manya looked at him when she reached for the sketch. Chaim sucked in another breath, grabbed his sister's shoulder, and said in a clear voice, "You. This is you."

Manya began to cry and dance at the same time. She spun and twirled and threw her Kipling into the air.

"You, this is you," Chaim said again, first speaking, then singing out each word as he pointed to the sketch, then Manya.

"Stay here, please," she told him. "I'll get everyone." And just to be certain she wasn't dreaming, she called to her brother from the edge of the wood. "Whose face is it, Chaim?" she asked.

"You, this is you," he answered.

At the same moment Manya Turkow began racing home, the Jewish elders of Nowy Dwor were sipping their scalding lemon tea in Moishe Turkow's dining hall. Lipe Shvager, the only Jewish lawyer in Nowy Dwor allowed to practice his profession in the local courts, was angrily denouncing the policies and diatribes of some comical politician in Germany who, though an Austrian by birth, had brought his hatred of Jews and Slavs to Germany along with his citizenship. No one in the dining hall paid too much attention to Court Counselor Shvager's display of newspaper clippings from the Warsaw dailies or to his long-winded explanations. Moishe Turkow was just about to say of his friend's Austrian nemesis, "A fool like that blows away in the wind," but he never got the chance, because Manya Turkow burst through the dining hall's swinging doors, stamping her feet while pointing toward the river.

Moishe, of course, thought the worst had happened — a drowning victim had washed ashore, or the Poles had started a revolution, or, God forbid, one of his daughters had been attacked by a peasant. Still, given Manya's hysterical expression and her inability to explain her outrageous behavior, there was nothing to do but follow the speechless girl and see for himself. It's never good, he thought, to be inside when trouble comes.

With Manya charging toward the Narew twenty meters ahead of him, Moishe, along with six or seven other Jews brave enough to view what surely must be an awful sight, ran through the main street of Nowy Dwor to the road that led to the river. The innkeeper lost sight of his daughter, and also his footing, when she took an unfamiliar path through the thick woods, but he recovered his bearings when he finally heard her yell his name. "I'm coming, little one," he shouted. By this point Moishe knew there must be a corpse floating along the mud-soaked shoreline. "Don't touch anything!"

No answer. Moishe and his army pushed ahead until, after clearing away the last branch blocking their view, they arrived together to see Manya Turkow standing next to her brother. "Now, Chaim," Manya said. "Tell him. Tell all of them!"

Chaim waved to his exhausted father. He bowed to the respected and panting elders whose boots were covered with dirt and leaves. He held up his sketch, which he'd changed slightly by adding his father's image, showing him walking in front of the little elephant (and wearing a towel). And then, before anyone could embrace him, he opened his mouth wide enough to be heard over the sound of Moishe Turkow's gasping and his sister's laughter.

3

WHILE EVERY JEW in Nowy Dwor knew that Moishe Turkow regained his faith at the exact moment when Chaim spoke, and that Manya now accepted the place of miracles in this world, it was left to the rabbi to tell the truth.

"Listen, Moishe," he said after the innkeeper complained that Chaim showed no interest in becoming a scholar, "understand this — your son came back to you because of a few pieces of colored chalk and a goyische writer." (Chaim carried the Kipling book everywhere, much to the rabbi's horror.) "God made it happen this way for a reason. So be satisfied to give the boy paper, enough Hebrew to pray with you every morning, and a love for Torah."

Moishe thought about what the rabbi had advised, though it hurt him to accept such counsel only one year after Chaim's remarkable recovery. But Moishe Turkow knew how quickly a Jew could lose what he loved. And he did not wish to anger the demons who waited for the slightest hint that one was weak. Finally, after a particularly frustrating attempt to share some of Rashi's commentaries with the boy, Moishe decided to give up his plan to return his son to a life devoted exclusively to God's teachings. Still, it wasn't easy for Moishe to watch his son lose interest so quickly — Chaim's eyes strayed from any text after a few minutes — and the well-meant consolation of the innkeeper's friends did little to ease his pain. "The boy will be righteous in other ways," they told him. "In time, how can he avoid having our wisdom dribble through his heart?" Moishe Turkow, however, was not appeased.

But what should he do? What would become of a boy who, though almost as tall as his father, doodled on the endpapers of prayerbooks, on tabletops, even (this, Moishe saw for himself on numerous occasions) in the dust of Nowy Dwor's unpaved streets — and all coming, Moishe thought, from a boy whose beauty still caused Poles as well as Jews to stare at him long after he passed by them. "A Polish noble," the Turkows' Catholic maid said to her friends, "has been mistakenly dropped in a Jew's house. Maybe he's a prince with bad luck!"

Lena Turkow was more practical. "Go for a swim," she suggested to her husband after he spent another sleepless night thinking about the son who would never become a rabbi. "The water has always helped you before."

So, Moishe Turkow swam — six days a week for an entire month, churning the green water of the Narew with his strong legs past peasant fishermen who laughed and even threw stones at the bubbles he left in his wake. With each stroke, Moishe presented God with his problem, only to feel the solution give way to another problem, another question even more difficult than its predecessor. With each kick of his heavy legs, he thought he had the answer, and soon finding himself bobbing like a cork in the middle of the river, he began to wonder whether it was only the Jews who were afflicted by such incessant, troubled questioning. Chaim as innkeeper? No; the boy was too shy to trade jokes and riddles with salesmen and drunken Poles or to barter over spoiled vegetables with peasants. A shopowner with, say, leather goods brought in from Warsaw? Never; he'd lose track of his accounts within a fortnight. Chaim as ritual slaughterer with enough guaranteed business to attract a bride who'd bring along a substantial dowry? Impossible; the boy had no use for such a blood-sotted life under the strict tutelage of someone like Mordcha Rostzat, not to mention the years he'd have to spend learning the laws that went hand-in-hand with the knife. And as far as some sort of commercial clerkship with a reputable moneylender was concerned, Moishe was wise enough to see his son's mind withering under a constant onslaught of figures and interest payments.

Exhausted, upset, his head soaked through to the brain, the innkeeper finally pulled himself atop a log raft some thirty or so meters from the shore. He lay on the logs with his stomach pressed against the raft's smooth, slimy surface. Bookseller? Scribe or tanner? Teacher?

Then, not far from where his raft settled with a jolt into the riverbank, Moishe heard his children's voices coming from a vine-covered glade.

"You have to *feel* the colors before you draw," Chaim was saying to his sister.

"It's warm . . . yes, I feel it . . . it's warm like Mama's best summer blouse, the one with the red trim," Manya Turkow answered. "Can I try the yellow chalk now?"

From his hidden spot on the log raft, Moishe expertly (and quietly) paddled to within a few meters of his children. He pushed aside an overhanging willow branch and spied Manya and Chaim as they both took their chalks, concentrating on their sketches as if there weren't any Poland, any Jews, or a failed Austrian artist waving at his adoring admirers — Chaim sometimes guiding his sister's hand, occasionally correcting her strokes with a slight push to the left or right.

"Good, just like that, Manya. Don't take your hand away from the paper. Smooth lines can be shaded with a wet finger to bring out a softer color."

Their former roles now reversed — Chaim as teacher, Manya the obedient student — the two youngest children of innkeeper Turkow intently translated Chaim's strange idea of color into a drawing of some wildflowers. Chaim finished before his sister, and held the paper up as an example. The sunlight shimmered through the drawing and made it glow, just like the stained-glass windows Moishe had once seen in one of Warsaw's great cathedrals.

And then, between the seconds when Chaim held Manya's sketch next to his own and Moishe Turkow let his head drop over the raft's side in gratitude, the innkeeper found his answer. He slipped off the raft into the warm water, kicked his legs like a demon chasing a pious Jew, and swam to a place where the two artists wouldn't be able to see the source of the churning water. He fumbled with the buttons of the shirt and pants he'd hidden beneath an old religious shrine of the Virgin. He dressed without completely drying himself.

It must have been a sight to see the innkeeper running through the back streets of Nowy Dwor, water dripping from his hair, shirt half unbuttoned, skullcap sticking to his forehead like an ill-positioned handbill on a kiosk. "Make way," he shouted to the giggling Jewish women who pointed to the innkeeper's backward trousers. "Make way!" To the Polish peasants who were setting up their stalls in the marketplace, Moishe changed languages: "I'm in a hurry, friends, so make way!" Neither the catcalls of the peasants' children who tried to grab his sopping coat, nor the piercing whistles of Nowy Dwor's yeshiva boys on their morning break from Talmud study, stopped the innkeeper from reaching his destination — for we all know that when someone has found the solution, petty details of proper behavior and dress are of no real significance. Besides, Moishe Turkow had to find Milutsky, the only Jew in Nowy Dwor who could help him find a life for his son. "Make way, please," Moishe Turkow shouted. "I need some room."

Luck was with him on the short journey to the side street where Jacob Schmul Milutsky, Nowy Dwor's only master printer and engraver (offering studio photography as an additional service), held court for his friends and customers on the solid wooden benches in front of his shop.

"Jacob, Jacob," Moishe shouted, his chest heaving from the exertion of so much excitement and understanding. "Take my son as an apprentice. The boy knows colors!"

Jacob Schmul Milutsky — master printer, Zionist of long standing, a socialist who could admire Bakunin as well as Marx, a painter of oversized watercolors devoted to Biblical themes, amateur playwright and occasional Yiddish poet who read his lines and verses to the more progressive secularists in Nowy Dwor, and, as he liked to brag to his more gullible comrades, a former youthful lover of Rosa Luxemburg herself — gladly shook the wet outstretched hand of the breathless innkeeper. No one was deprived of the hand of Milutsky, not even those who still relied on religious superstition and a life given over to a very fickle deity!

"And what will you have me make of him, Reb Moishe?" he asked in a joking manner. "A devout signpainter?"

Moishe removed an irritating strand of river weed that had lodged in his ear and, caring little about his baffling appearance or the stares of Milutsky's anarchist friends, collapsed without apologizing next to the notorious atheist (but very good brewer) Grossmann.

"Teach him to be a printer, Jacob. Give him a steady hand."

Through the smoke of the French cigarettes that followed him like a permanent cloud, the master printer studied Moishe's face while he listened to the story. Moishe, of course, omitted nothing at all: there was the "miracle" and the boy's birth, the prayers Chaim knew even before he could walk ten paces by himself, Hebrew and Aramaic and Talmud by three years, the rabbi who never came from Bialystok, the bathhouse steam, the terrible years of silence, an English storyteller, a daughter's lessons that brought her brother back to God's earth, and all the swimming that Moishe had suffered over the years (not to mention the earaches and assorted fevers). When he finished — Moishe ending with the wildflowers of recent memory — Jacob Schmul Milutsky had already made his decision as to the probable future of the golden-haired son of Moishe Turkow.

But there was one condition.

"What will I derive from such a proposed relationship, Reb Turkow?"

"A thousand zloty, paid over ten months. Is this enough?" Moishe choked out.

"No."

"More?"

"No money, Reb Turkow — not a groschen."

Moishe felt yet another solution flying into the dust. "Then what can I give?"

Milutsky shooed away the loyal retainers who kept up a steady hum of amusement over the course of Milutsky's affairs with the Observant innkeeper. Above all, the printer didn't want tongues wagging when they contemplated the results of the *only* payment he, Jacob Schmul Milutsky, would ever exact from a Jew as Torah-true as Moishe Turkow. He bent closer to the innkeeper and spoke in a low voice.

"It's simple, Reb Turkow. Just let the boy grow both in my world and in your own. Without your word on this, I'll do nothing for him — or you!"

Moishe Turkow closed his eyes and willed himself back to the log raft on the river Narew. He weighed his decision as carefully as he might count a month's receipts from the inn: clerk, tanner, butcher on one side of his mental ledger; printer made out of a doodler and flower-lover on the opposite side. The risks were great, and Moishe Turkow knew how much he was giving up to this middle-aged worldly purveyor of radical politics, whose exploits in Warsaw and Krakow made a good Jew cringe. But Moishe loved his son and, truth to tell, he couldn't dismiss the memory of the Warsaw cathedrals and their stained-glass renderings of a dewy-eyed Jesus.

"But will you," Moishe finally asked, but only after he fell to his knees before the startled printer, "let him wear a hat and send him home before sundown every Friday?"

Milutsky, in keeping with his notions of social equality, joined the innkeeper knee-to-knee in the small puddle of Narew water. "I am a Jew, Reb Turkow, perhaps not the kind you'd like, but a Jew all the same. I would never deny another kind of Jew his schul within four walls, even though my faith comes from without. Chaim Turkow will wear his skullcap. He will always be at your door well before Shabbos candles

are lit, but he will let a bit of different light into his head, too,
and —"

"And?" Moishe interrupted, fearing the worst to come.

"*And* he will learn to have a steady hand. Is this promise
enough for you?"

Moishe nodded; Milutsky offered his hand. And that's how
it came about that Chaim Turkow, adored son of Lena and
Moishe, celebrated his fourteenth birthday on the morrow
with three gifts: a gilt-edged edition of the late Rabbi Ayzik
Fayvlovitsch's commentaries on mysticism, offered by Chaim's
ever-hopeful parents; an ornately inscribed document, written
by Milutsky himself, stating that Chaim Ben Moishe was now
apprenticed to the "studio and workshop of Master Printer and
Engraver Jacob Schmul Milutsky"; and, from Manya Turkow,
a sketchbook. "To the teacher who came out from the castle,"
she wrote on the inside cover, "and taught me about a flower's
color."

✦ ✦ ✦

The next day, father and son arrived at Milutsky's shop a full
hour before it was due to open. Despite Moishe Turkow's op-
timism, Chaim was nervous, had no idea what to expect from
Milutsky, and couldn't imagine what led his father to think
that he, Chaim, had any aptitude for the drudgery of the
printer's trade. "So you'll learn," Moishe Turkow kept saying.
"These flower sketches of yours won't earn you a groschen, but
the posters and handbills Milutsky will teach you to make will
bring you zloty, respect, and maybe even a shop of your own.
There will always be Poles and Jews in Nowy Dwor who want
to read their messages and have their pictures taken!" To prove
his point, Moishe Turkow insisted on reading the sign that

swayed above Milutsky's door. "It took courage to write that, Chaim, but think of the importance of a sign that says ETERNAL MEMORIES ON ANY SIZE PAPER (REASONABLE RATES)."

Master Printer Milutsky couldn't have been happier to see his new apprentice admiring the sign. He greeted Chaim and made a polite bow to the innkeeper. "Enough stargazing, gentlemen," he said, "there's work to be done today." Milutsky's businesslike attitude and forceful manner impressed Moishe, especially the way he explained all of the orders he needed to finish ("with perfect attention to detail!") before midday.

"Seven hundred posters in all, Reb Turkow, not to mention the photographs I promised to make of Reb Finkel's daughters. So just think how much time it takes to set type, ink the rollers, and, if you'll forgive me, the effort involved in making the daughters of David Finkel look like Solomon's wives!"

Moishe made a quick calculation of the income Finkel's patronage would bring, and he was pleased with the results. He patted his son on the back. "For the promise of fifty zloty earned before supper, don't waste Reb Milutsky's time with your foolish sketching."

Before Moishe Turkow left, Milutsky called for his "shop assistant," Jerzy Fiatkowski. Moishe flinched when he saw the Catholic youth medal pinned to the young man's stained vest and the broad Slavic face and forehead that made him a true son of Poland. "Ah, not to be alarmed, Reb Turkow," Milutsky said. "This is a Polish brother who loves us well. He speaks his own language better than a landowner and our Yiddish like a Warsaw poet. Then, turning to the collection of hand-painted postcards displayed on a nearby wall, "Our Jerzy's work," the printer proudly announced, slapping Jerzy on the back. Moishe couldn't help noticing the Pole's interest in picturing scenes from the poorer sections of Nowy Dwor. "The world is not all beautiful," Milutsky said to the innkeeper. "Poor Jews, poor Poles, eh, Reb Turkow?"

Jerzy Fiatkowski welcomed the Turkows in perfect Yiddish. Since he was well versed in all the political and social gossip he overheard in the company of Milutsky's more progressive friends, the Pole was about to give the details of "a little tale having to do with Finkel's most buxom daughter," the very one, he added, "who wore her blouses like a singer," when Milutsky reappeared with a box filled with ink bottles of all sizes. The Turkows watched the master printer hovering over the bottles, inspecting one after another as if, Jerzy whispered to Moishe Turkow, they were holy water (the mention of which made the innkeeper grow red and sweaty). Finally, satisfied with a bottle he held up to the light, Milutsky motioned to his new apprentice.

"Take it in your hands. For now we begin learning about my first principle."

With Jerzy's help Chaim put on a heavy cloth apron that bore the tinted fingerprints from many different posters. Then Milutsky attached a leather strap to both ends of the box of bottles and lowered it over Chaim Turkow's head. "First principle, first rule," Milutsky continued. "This box pulling against your neck can make people live forever! Understood?"

"Yes."

"Then repeat, please."

"This box," a nervous Chaim Turkow said, without looking at Milutsky, "can make people live forever."

Printer Milutsky smiled and turned Chaim around so that his father could see him. "He now knows the first commandment of Milutsky's business, Reb Turkow. So, with your permission, we printers will now have something to eat to celebrate the moment."

Milutsky busied himself lighting the old brass samovar that took up an entire corner of the shop. Jerzy Fiatkowski brought out a tray piled high with sweet biscuits and a single lemon cut into thin wedges. When the samovar boiled and shot its rich, fragrant steam toward Milutsky's face, Jerzy Fiatkowski politely offered the largest glass to the only blue-eyed Jew he'd ever seen.

"Do your blessings, apprentice Turkow," Milutsky said, winking at the innkeeper. "An artisan's word is worth everything. Have your breakfast here and say good-bye to your father, and in fifteen minutes I'll start to teach you how to follow my rules for the rest of your life."

Moishe Turkow bent to inspect the biscuits. "Are these fit for my son?"

Milutsky laughed and took the innkeeper's hand. "Fresh today, Reb Turkow — and everything from the blessed ovens of the most pious baker in Nowy Dwor, a Hasid of the highest standing! And we do wish you, sir, a good and prosperous day at your inn."

Moishe nodded and, though he never remembered putting on his coat, was soon outside the printer's shop. Just to be sure of his son's welfare, he waited by the window where Milutsky displayed samples of his printing and photography, including at least a dozen photographs of young women in wedding dresses, and watched Chaim dutifully offer a blessing before he bit into the biscuit. Milutsky's lips, he noticed, moved in time with Chaim's blessing, although the printer was hatless ("Forgive him, Lord," Moishe said aloud). Jerzy Fiatkowski crossed himself. Moishe groaned at the sight of such an ecumenical gathering in front of his son. After he folded Chaim's apprenticeship papers and raised his eyes toward the cloudless autumn sky, Moishe Turkow — certainly a good man for all of his worrying — made one more request. "Let my boy remain a good Jew, even" — here, Moishe had to struggle with the last few words — "even if he has to learn from someone who takes photographs of women who don't wear wigs!"

✦ ✦ ✦

Not more than an hour after Chaim Turkow's anxious father left him alone with Milutsky and the Yiddish-speaking Pole, Chaim was staring at a nude figure in one of Milutsky's art manuals — preparation, he was told, for knowing how to make the occasional "fancy sketch" sometimes necessary for a "special order." "But say nothing to your parents," the printer warned him. "For I doubt if they would understand my second principle: Know the body before you ever pick up a pencil or a sliver of chalk."

Jerzy, sensing the boy's embarrassment, sat next to Chaim and was encouraging in his singsong Yiddish. "Don't worry about it, you'll never see Finkel's daughters looking like that!"

Almost as if Milutsky had prearranged a stage entrance, the brass bells hanging above the door rang out to announce the entrance of Finkel and his seven daughters. The printer smiled at each girl, kissed their pudgy and sweaty hands, and offered his warmest handshake to the proud father.

"Over here, ladies," Jerzy called. "The sofa awaits."

Like seven portly ducklings chasing one another on a not-too-sturdy riverbank, Finkel's girls fussed over one another's hair as they shuffled along, giggled at Milutsky's mock anger when they didn't sit straight or chattered too much, but then clapped when Jerzy brought out the large painted backdrop that was about to frame their ample bodies within a colorful Venetian scene.

"I painted each gondola myself," Milutsky boasted to the wealthy man. "But this shimmering landscape never enjoyed such company before."

Chaim Turkow stood behind Milutsky while the printer changed a lens on his expensive German portrait camera. He wiped the glass with a soft cloth. When all was ready, he inserted a glass plate that would soon capture the daughters Finkel for all time. Beckoning his new apprentice to join him under the black drape that hung from the back of the camera, Milutsky was breathing hard and trying not to laugh at the image of the girls, hanging upside down in sharp focus, their legs attached to a wave in the Grand Canal. "Nothing is wide enough to get in all of this lot," he whispered about the newly installed Italian ladies of Nowy Dwor. At the last second, Milutsky inserted a wide-angle lens at the front of his camera.

"I count to three, Chaim, and then you pop up and throw them a little kiss. Believe me, they'll love it when they see my yeshiva boy making advances."

Chaim smacked his lips in time, loudly enough for furrier Finkel to be a bit taken aback by such boldness and resulting in a sincere assurance from the printer to the good merchant that everything was being done solely "for the sake of art and your daughters' future husbands."

It was also for the sake of art, as well as to celebrate the generous payment given by Reb David Finkel, that Milutsky later brought out a small bottle of vodka after the long, tiring session. He poured the clear liquid into three tiny glasses. "To our new comrade, a happy future," Milutsky beamed.

As befitted his station in the shop of Jacob Schmul Milutsky, Chaim returned the toast with one of his own (this after the fourth drink), one he'd frequently heard when his father's dining hall was crowded with Polish tradesmen. "And may you live a hundred years," he said in Polish to a slightly tipsy Jerzy Fiatkowski. "Not a second less."

Their friendship and camaraderie sealed forever, Milutsky cleared away the vodka and asked Chaim to attend to the task of bringing forth the images of Finkel's daughters from the glass plates "so that our work will result in all of them capturing good Jewish husbands, fat babies, and full ovens."

Closing the door behind them, Milutsky worked and instructed at the same time. Solutions with strange names in certain trays, chemicals in another. Precise adjustments of the enlarger that hung over the glass plates like a hungry vulture. One hour into their labor under the reddish glow necessary for such work, Milutsky, his small hands encased in rubber gloves, stepped back from the table and sighed as if an important moment had just arrived.

"Now for the magic, Chaim Turkow. After all, who but a master could even try to turn the zaftig daughters of David Finkel into lovely Venetian ladies who just happen to be visiting a warmer place than Poland?"

4

ON A RAINY November day in 1938, only one year after Chaim Turkow became the best apprentice printer and poster artist Jacob Schmul Milutsky had ever employed, Moishe Turkow was, for a short time, certain that the devil (or perhaps one of his lesser minions) had come to Nowy Dwor. And though Moishe never stopped loving God after this day, he began to think of the Blessed One as an older brother who sometimes made a few mistakes in his grand scheme for creation. "Swimming in cold river water," he told Mordcha Rostzat, "won't be able to help me anymore."

✦ ✦ ✦

From the beginning Moishe Turkow had followed every step of his son's training at Milutsky's shop. He visited the master printer whenever there was a slack period at the inn, offered Milutsky business advice, occasionally inked the printing press while his son was busy with Milutsky in the back room, and generously placed orders for posters he didn't need. He even listened to the master printer lecture his son and the Pole about fascism within and without Poland. For his part, Milutsky kept his solemn promise to Reb Turkow: Chaim continued to live as an Observant Jew, he was always given time off to celebrate the many religious holidays (Moishe had sent Milutsky a calendar, with each major and minor holiday circled in red), and, no matter how much work lay on his bench, Chaim always felt free to become the tenth man for an emergency minyan. "Go, go," the printer told his apprentice, "never be late to help the believers. But if you have a moment, why not make a few pencil sketches of the other nine Jews."

Moishe Turkow did not, however, understand that his son's outward piety was like the first layer of paint over a canvas — pleasant to look at, yet not the truth. For, although Milutsky was contracted to teach what he knew of the printer's craft to Chaim Turkow, it was to his "other loves," as he told Chaim, that he owed his greatest loyalty. "To Art, yeshiva boy . . . always to Art."

Milutsky — painter of oversized watercolors, a printer turned sketch artist — would, at any hour, call for Chaim Turkow to come and join him on one of his long walks away from the shop. Notebook in hand, pencils or charcoals carried in a wooden case attached to a long string tied to his jacket button, he taught the innkeeper's son how to quickly draw the iron railings outside the homes of Nowy Dwor's bourgeoisie, the broken sheds the peasants used to store their carts, the old men reading Yiddish newspapers, the Jewish women haggling with street vendors. Or there was Milutsky the lover of Russian poetry, recalling from memory a fragment from Blok or Pushkin, or even the young Pasternak ("His father was a very decent painter, you know," Milutsky told everyone. "He knew Tolstoy himself!"). His voice raw from cigarettes and brandy, he shouted verses across the empty market square or in Nowy Dwor's only coffeehouse. And, of course, Milutsky the engraver, printer of posters, handbills, and broadsides for any number of Zionist groups, who demanded of Chaim Turkow only that he practice his drawing and pay attention to whatever Milutsky said about life, God, politics, and the Palestine the printer had only imagined in his paintings and dreams.

So talented was this young apprentice of Milutsky's, so quickly did he learn the theory and practice of the art chosen for him (Milutsky always spoke about their "art," never their "profession"), that the master printer allowed Chaim more and more freedom to experiment and work on his own. Within a few months the innkeeper's son was weaned away from the more routine printing jobs and given his own working space, where he drew charcoal outlines for the new backdrops Milutsky used to charm and soothe his studio photography customers. By the end of his first year, Chaim began painting huge murals depicting Milutsky's favorite Italian scenes — the master printer finally conceded Chaim's greater skills at drawing gondolas and Venetian canalscapes — and panoramic views of Jerusalem in reddish and golden hues. "You can stay with me for life, if you want," Milutsky told Chaim nearly every morning after they opened the shop. "After all, I know God commanded us to make good art, and since I'm as good a Jew as anyone here, we will follow this law for life. Now, to work!"

Their painting was usually done by midmorning. Though it meant that he frequently called for a new run of posters at the last moment, Milutsky never let any piece of work leave the shop until it was perfect. But once satisfied, he insisted that his two workers share a tea break together — Chaim on a low stool by his table, Jerzy Fiatkowski balancing his glass and sweet rolls on top of the press, eating with one hand and using the other to clean or oil some strange gear only the Pole could locate. Jacob would spend the next few hours at the shop and leave only after he was certain that Chaim was concentrating on what he called "his jewel time of the day." You see, Milutsky insisted that Moishe Turkow's son spend part of his day studying with him, always the same subjects: Polish grammar and literature (especially poetry), basic drawing and human anatomy, the history of Western art (he never got past Goya) with examples taken from his expensive collection of reproductions, and, finally, "writing lessons" in two languages. "If you want to be a thief and steal images from the world," he liked to say, "then it's best you understand something about the house you've broken into."

With his fingers stained from the exotic colors ("Bombay Blue" and "Flower of the Gold Coast" being his favorites) that he used to illustrate his own poetry and plays, Milutsky would prance around his shop like a teacher running out of time before the last bell of the day.

✦ ✦ ✦

Moishe Turkow couldn't have been more pleased with his son's progress at Milutsky's. But he still maintained a constant vigil over Chaim's spiritual health, fearful lest the boy fall into the secular traps set by Milutsky. The printer's world, Moishe Turkow reasoned, was replete with demented ideas about government, social justice, and a revisionist cosmopolitanism beloved by secular Zionists. Playing the role of the interested father (Milutsky often referred to his apprentice's father as "the living rod of justice"), the innkeeper often lingered at the shop, taking a seat beside his son while the printer read aloud from his verse and plays. "Too long,"

Moishe might say when asked his opinion of a poem or a few lines of dialogue. "Study more Talmud, Jacob, then you'll know everything!" or "Put the Law into your writing before it's too late."

Milutsky would always turn to the innkeeper and smile. "I'll get to the Law if you read Herzl," he said, winking at Chaim. "Not a moment before."

And so it was on that November morning that Reb Turkow, his son, and Jerzy Fiatkowski were party to a "preliminary reading" of the latest Milutsky creation, a one-act play intended, the printer said, for the Jewish children of Nowy Dwor. "I have in mind now — now listen carefully — doing something with Genesis," Jacob said.

Ever on guard, Moishe Turkow was prepared. "Genesis! How can you possibly make truth like that come to a stage, Jacob? First of all, you won't be able to use many characters, unless you have the fish speaking. Or maybe the rocks and sky can add a bit of dialogue, eh?" But when Moishe looked at his son's employer he saw how serious he was.

"No, no, you don't understand. I can have characters by letting everything that is created speak. Why not? Let the children give life to rocks and lizards. Clear?"

Milutsky walked to the center of the large room and kicked aside wooden boxes and bound satchels of posters. He begged a moment to give a brief "demonstration." Dragging a ladder from the storage closet, he set it next to Jerzy. "Get the rolls of cloth from the shed," he told the Pole. "I need some clouds."

Milutsky disappeared into the closet where he stored inks and chemicals for the darkroom. He pulled out a stepladder and set it in the middle of the room.

"Quiet, all of you. Close your eyes. You have to imagine

the stage set with brown and green cloth covering the floor. Smoke will drift in from the wings, and a small backlight will refect through this haze.. Now, open your eyes, my friends, and behold!"

Such a sight: Milutsky perched over the ladder, holding on to the rungs, covered by a large blanket, a black cord drooping from his backside like a serpent's tail. His one uncovered arm held an electric switch attached to the cord, which ran across the room to an old lamp.

"Let there be . . . be . . ." Milutsky yanked on the cord.

" 'Light,' Reb Jacob," Jerzy cried. "It's 'light'!"

With one quick jerk, Milutsky pulled the switch and the lamp was blazing, its white glare showing everything with the help of a powerful new bulb.

God's amorphous shape began to move — and groan. Milutsky was punching the sides of the blanket with every ooh and ahh.

"This I shall call the day that I have made. What more can I make for the place I am creating?" the blanketed deity shouted. "And this part" — God's left arm rose within the blanket until it pointed toward a bewildered Moishe Turkow — "I shall divide into the darkness.

"God's voice will come from over here," Milutsky continued, "I will have this voice drift around the room by wandering over the stage. His voice will be everywhere — 'Ooh . . . ooh, what a place I have made. What more, I ask you, can I make for this sweet world I am bringing together?'" Milutsky's God asked, " ' For I am surely excited by all of this business!' "

"My children will be hiding beneath flowing pieces of blue or brown cloth: blue for the water, brown for the land. Watch how this will happen. First, God's lines: 'Ooh, but it is time to bring all of this together, to make this world I have thought about for so long.' "

Moishe Turkow was now beside himself, wailing like Job. "It takes a lot of chutzpah to revise Genesis the way you've done, Jacob Milutsky! You expect our children to watch this travesty of the Holy Word?"

Milutsky threw off his blanket. "Atmosphere, my Turkow. Atmosphere and mystery. Can't you imagine what the children will feel when they see God, so powerful and good, wanting to make a world? He creates things. Rocks and dust and trees and even worms. Birds in the air and stalking beasts. Even fruit and tiny seeds are indebted to him."

Milutsky jumped to the firmament and walked over each section of the shop-floor-become-stage and pointed. "Here, I will have little Sora Gittleman as a rock along with her sister and fellow rock, Rive-Mindl. And there, by your son's foot, Reb Turkow, Dovid Sosnowsky will become a seed who will join other seeds, like Yosel Sukenik and Moishe Strayber. And maybe if I talk sweetly to her I can convince Nokmen Aizer's tiny daughter, the one with the bad leg, to be one of our stars. Wonderful: that lovely little Sara sitting on the stage with a light, a blue light, shining in front of her silver costume.

"Think of it, Turkow, maybe even one of your own grand-children — you who tell them about Zion every night before they go to sleep — think of your Rachel's son Leybel as a bird adorned with peacock feathers. Why, by the fifth day your grandson will be created and thanking God by flying above the firmament. Won't he be excited? Won't he move with joy?"

Moishe Turkow collapsed, speechless, into his seat. He stared at his son. I've made a great mistake, he thought. My son has been working with a madman!

"There's just one thing that puzzles me, Moishe Turkow," Milutsky said, suddenly looking helpless. "I need your advice."

The innkeeper's hands were wet. He felt his temple throbbing, his hands straining against his mind's order to thrash this demented secularist. Yet, just as one is required to give alms to the hungry and pity to a lame beggar, one owes sympathy to a *meshuge* — the Jew's sad, hard duty!

Milutsky jabbed a finger at one of the more soiled pages pages from his script. "It's so puzzling. Notice how I have copied the exact text from the Genesis chapter in order to understand that last verse. Listen: 'And God saw everything he had made, and, behold, *it was very good.*' Apply your mind to this, Moishe Turkow, and tell me the meaning. Look at the text again: *it was.* Did he intend his work to be past tense?"

"Past tense!" Moishe yelled. "What do you think has been going on for six days, Milutsky? He's done everything. *Everything.*"

Milutsky looked like a cheder boy who'd come across a new letter of the Hebrew alphabet for the first time. "Is it possible that God was beginning to worry about the results? Maybe he thought, What I've done was good, but who knows what will happen after this!"

Moishe Turkow's head drooped down to his knees. What he was hearing was beyond blasphemy, bordering on lunacy. "It *was* good," Moishe Turkow answered. "It still *is* good, Milutsky. How can you see a problem within a pool of such clear water?"

Milutsky, however, began to read from his several versions of the play's final scene. With each reading God became more and more sullen. The playwright was not one to withhold the appropriate stage directions, either: "God shakes his ladder, kicks at his crate, refuses to listen to the pleas of his creatures; even the rocks' attempts to address him are to no avail. He doesn't want rainbows. He shouts, 'You were so good, my creations, but consider what the future holds for you.' "

"Enough!" Moishe yelled. "Enough!"

Moishe Turkow tore the script away from Milutsky and searched for the offensive passages. Then he climbed the ladder that, only moments before, was home to Milutsky's now-uncertain God.

"I want you to picture this," Moishe said. "I am calm, so you please listen. As you first wrote it, God makes the world, while children play the roles of living things. Rocks, land, water, birds, are in place. Our Lord on a ladder smiles from his heaven. He 'oohs' because everything has gone so well. What could be better? Here is a loving God, the very same one who, in his mystery, somehow called upon Jacob Schmul Milutsky in Nowy Dwor to make water and rocks and lizards out of children and pieces of decorated paper. But then what do we finally get from the fiery pen of this same Milutsky? This, this!" Moishe steadied his trembling hands long enough to read from the script:

"And the light will shine upon all I have made, but, ooh, is it all so good? Will it remain forever as I have dreamed it?

(*God lifts a child to his shoulders, looks worried; his voice gets louder*)

"What will happen to you who are so new and good in the time I make?

(Lights dim and out; children bow, some cry)"

Moishe Turkow dropped the script on the floor. He looked at Milutsky. "This *dreck* you cannot tell children," he shouted, pointing a finger at the printer.

The innkeeper stalked out without a parting word to his son or the madman. I've put an end to it he thought. No more, ever!

And it was in such a black mood that Moishe Turkow, a righteous and God-fearing Jew, stopped at the studyhouse to lose himself in a commentary on the Gemara, finding a page where, he was certain, the world could be made right and just until the Messiah finally returned.

✦ ✦ ✦

Several hours later, after drinking many cups of lemon tea with the rabbi and arguing over an obscure point of the Law, Moishe Turkow heard some commotion in the street. A few men raised their voices outside the studyhouse, and within a few minutes most of the Jews holding tractates or commentaries had to find out what had happened.

But before Moishe Turkow could follow the others, a breathless Mordcha Rostzat, followed by his twin sons, burst into the quiet of God's studyhouse. The butcher waved a soiled Warsaw newspaper.

"They've started to burn the synagogues in Germany," he yelled. "Some Jewish kid from Poland shot a German diplomat in Paris."

Moishe Turkow took the newspaper, now as thin from handling as the membrane of a holiday carp. He read the names to himself and stared at the blurry photograph of a burning synagogue, a street covered by glass shards, and a frightened-looking child staring at the camera from a store window that had been painted over by a large *J*. The child's face, Moishe saw, was peeking over the bottom curve of the white letter.

The distraught innkeeper left his books and tea, ran from the studyhouse without a word; already he was thinking how he would tell his son that maybe Jacob Schmul Milutsky was right after all. The master printer should show the children what the world was like at the *beginning* of time, he muttered to himself like an actor practicing his lines — because (God forgive Moishe Turkow) the Blessed One wasn't doing so well for his chosen people to the west of Nowy Dwor.

✦ ✦ ✦

Three weeks later, with his Uncle Chaim working a rope attached to a pulley nailed into the ceiling of the Zionist Hall, Leybel Rappaport finally learned to fly.

5

ON A LOW GREEN HILL overlooking the Narew River, the twelve-year-old twins of Mordcha Rostzat watched the column of vehicles turn onto the dirt road from the west. Although the bright September sun nearly blinded them, both boys could still see the tiny clouds of dust that followed the trucks as they slowed down to avoid the holes no one had ever bothered to repair. Adam Rostzat, senior to his brother, Meyer, by two minutes, crawled behind an up-turned wagon and focused his toy telescope on the first truck.

Meyer nudged his brother. "How many are there?"

"Shush, pest, they're singing," Adam replied as he crawled to another spot. Being the elder of the two, he wanted to take in everything.

Raising his hands in a kind of victory salute, one of the soldiers unfurled a large flag, pointed it toward the narrow road, and began singing in a language that sounded vaguely familiar to anyone who grew up speaking Yiddish in Nowy Dwor.

"They seem to be very happy," Adam whispered to the brother who was still begging for a chance to watch the parade for himself. "I think they want to be here."

"Polish cavalry units?"

"Shush or I'll smack your face!" Then Adam moved down the hill a bit to hear more of the soldiers' song, while his brother, anxious to be a man, too, stood up and waved at the soldiers, who seemed, even from a nearby hill, to have so much energy.

At the same time that Mordcha Rostzat's sons were fighting for a chance to share the one toy telescope, the elders of Nowy Dwor's Jewish community had already assembled in front of the Pilsudski monument in the center of the old marketplace square. The nine men stood nervously in their best suits, having spent the morning with Moishe Turkow in the bathhouse, where, it was agreed, the new rulers of Poland would be greeted with courtesy and dignity. "'Don't worry, I knew them during the first war," Mordcha Rostzat said. "Those Germans always bluff their intentions, and they usually get the mail delivered on time."

One hour passed. The shadow cast by the great marshal's bronze horse provided some relief from the sun. The rabbi had to sit down alongside the edge of the memorial fountain. He hated, as he told Mordcha Rostzat, to leave his wife alone at a time like this. "She can't stand the strain, but I told her to remember the Germans from the last war and the way their commandant brought us some flour for the holidays."

From one of the older houses that faced the square, someone had tuned a wireless set to the crackling Warsaw frequency, hoping, we may assume, to receive whatever late bulletins might still be coming from the besieged capital. "Tell that fool to smash his radio," Mordcha Rostzat yelled in the direction of the scratchy sound, but the radio continued to emit its low hum and Mordcha had to be content with the glass of vodka his shop assistant brought to him.

From his second-story workroom, just above the enticing printer's sign, Jacob Schmul Milutsky also watched and waited for the soldiers. Along with his two assistants, the printer had already checked, cleaned, and loaded several cameras. He'd spent hours finding just the right place for each of the cameras by the leaded windows that overlooked the square — each angle of approach taken into account, each possibility for capturing this historic day on film imagined before it happened. One camera, the small Leica, was securely fastened to a tripod, two others dangled like polished stones from Jerzy Fiatkowski's neck. Milutsky's instructions were clear, issued without emotion or excitement: Jerzy was to take photographs as soon as he heard the sound of motors from the west, while Milutsky himself would focus the Leica with the better lens on the nine Jewish elders, whose faces, he saw, were temporarily in the shadows. By the time Milutsky and the Pole settled into position next to each other, Chaim Turkow — wedged into a tight space one floor above them, in the attic where Milutsky stored his paintings — had removed the shutter and wooden slats that gave him a full view of his father and the other men. Chaim's legs were twisted and uncomfortable from trying to balance between several rafters smelling of mouse dung, but he could see everything and his hands were steady enough to sketch the first thin lines of two faces.

"Don't move," Chaim said, wanting to lean out the window and shout to Moishe Turkow, but any sudden movement and his legs might slip from the warped rafters. The pencils he'd brought were jumping too quickly over his paper: the rabbi's face unfinished before another hat or coat appeared on a different section of the sketchpad, Lipe Shvager's vest ring and Mordcha Rostzat's silver campaign buttons from the last war needing attention in yet another spot. The attic's heat and the stench of the mouse droppings made him dizzy; sweat soon poured from his forehead and a few drops fell onto the paper, making Mordcha Rostzat's ear blur. Once, twice, Milutsky knocked on the ceiling — his signal that Chaim should return three knocks if he, the best artist in Nowy Dwor, needed any fresh paper. "Yes, Papa, like that," Chaim kept saying. "Keep looking over here."

The bells from the church began to ring; two chickens ran across the square — present circumstances freeing them from the oven — and the irritating wireless set still buzzed. No one, it was remarked, could ever remember such a lovely autumn.

"If this is war," apothecary Adelstein said to Moishe Turkow, "then we might be safe after all. Maybe they'll take another road?" Moishe began to say something but drew closer to the statue when he saw the first truck approaching the only paved road in Nowy Dwor.

Slowly circling the eight Jews clustered around their rabbi, the first truck (the one with the flag) finally stopped at the far end of the square and waited for ten minutes before the other trucks, driving in a low, grinding gear, followed the same route in a wide circle around the elders. Without any command or signal, twelve young soldiers jumped down from each of the trucks and arranged themselves in a long, nearly perfect line across the entire square, their rifles slung across their shoulders with grace and symmetry. "Perfect discipline," Mordcha Rostzat whispered to innkeeper Turkow. "Just perfect." The innkeeper counted seventy-two soldiers before he realized that he'd wet himself.

An officer opened the door of the lead truck. Carefully

adjusting his cap with the tiny silver skull in the middle, the officer accepted a salute from the soldier to his immediate left. Moishe Turkow thought he heard the young officer say "Wait" to the same soldier who offered such a crisp salute. Apothecary Adelstein fell backward into the fountain and had to be pulled out by Moishe Turkow and Dovid Hendel, Moishe grateful that his shame was now covered by the water from the dripping apothecary.

"Names?" the officer asked, bowing in the rabbi's direction and speaking in unaccented Polish. "Please tell me your names and offices." The nine Jewish elders — one old rabbi, one lawyer, one apothecary, two lumber merchants, a butcher, two shopowners, and, of course, one innkeeper — likewise bowed to the pleasant officer. Slowly and loudly, as Poles are wont to do when they address someone who is not a native speaker, they gave their names and occupations.

The officer wrote down each Jew's name in a small notebook. He studied his work, comparing names with faces. Lipe Shvager was trying to remember how to conjugate a few German verbs when the officer put his notebook away and, still politely, said, "Jew Rostzat. Step forward, please."

Mordcha Rostzat — a former lance corporal in one of Pilsudski's famous cavalry units, which had turned back the Bolsheviks from Warsaw during Poland's late moment of glory — actually saluted the officer and puffed his chest out a bit to show his silver medals. He made a feeble attempt to click his heels together but lost his footing on the wet pavement. He was about to call out the name of his military unit when, despite the late afternoon haze and dust, he saw the trussed bodies of his twin sons being thrown through the rear flaps of the officer's truck, the battered heads of Adam and Meyer

Rostzat hitting the ground just a second before one of the soldiers shattered the toy spyglass at Mordcha Rostzat's feet. It was only then that the officer returned the salute so common in military life by clicking his own well-polished boots, making a sharp noise that hid the sound of two snapping camera shutters not more than seventy meters above the nine Jews, their new rulers, and the hum of the wireless set.

✦ ✦ ✦

By the light of a hissing kerosene lantern in the damp cellar of his printshop, Milutsky affixed each dripping photograph to the thin rope that ran across the length of the musty room. There was no ventilation, and the sickly-sweet smell of developing solution hung in the air like the heavy mist that followed springtime flooding of the river Narew. His assistants worked without talking and let the printer arrange the images in the order in which they'd been taken. But Milutsky wasn't quiet. "Here's the first truck that came into the square," he said, pointing a wet finger at the curling black and white print. "See how clearly you can make out their flag . . . and here, in this one, the officer is talking to the rabbi."

Chaim stood behind Milutsky and numbered the prints with special pencil, dating each soggy photograph and adding a few words of description. His hands shook. "And these five," Milutsky continued, "are the ones Jerzy took of Mordcha Rostzat and —"

"Say their names, Jacob," a voice in the corner shouted.

"— his two boys."

Moishe Turkow rose from the filthy floor where he had been sitting for the last hour. Although his leg ached terribly from the blows he had received from the young officer in the market square (Moishe had to be beaten away from Mordcha Rostzat with repeated kicks to the legs and chest), he still refused to wash Mordcha's blood from his own face and hands. He did, however, walk to Milutsky's studio without any assistance.

Dragging his bad leg behind him, Moishe Turkow stood next to his son for another look at the photographs showing how the war had come to the Jews of Nowy Dwor. "This is Mordcha Rostzat and his two boys, Jacob," he cried, reaching out for Chaim's hand to help steady himself in front of the swaying rope.

"Sha, sha, Moishe," Milutsky said. "We have to finish. Who knows how much time we have left before dawn. You can mourn after these other prints come out of the wash. Please, only two more left to prepare."

While Milutsky comforted the innkeeper, Jerzy Fiatkowski took over the job of rinsing the last few negatives until the image of Mordcha Rostzat's crumpled figure came into clear focus. The Pole crossed himself and turned away from the three Jews who stood by the tray. Chaim was breathing in short gasps.

"Ah, the sign, Milutsky said. "Now we can read!" Jerzy held the negative and inserted it into the enlarger, and despite the reverse nature of the negative image — black was white, white was black — the red bulb from the darkroom's light did not obscure the image of one of the soldiers tying a rope around the butcher's neck, nor did it hide the details of Mordcha Rostzat's final moment. " 'So, too, goes the father of Kike spies,' " Milutsky finally read on the sign attached to Mordcha's torn coat. "Ay! Quickly, now," he cautioned. "Blow on these. They're too wet to pack."

As Jerzy removed several prints from the drying rope and blew over several others, gently swinging these ill-smelling fans back and forth, Chaim covered his father's face. He didn't want Moishe to see the thick legs of Mordcha Rostzat dangling from the crossbar of the officer's truck. "Don't watch them like this, Papa. Not like this."

"Finished, Reb Milutsky," Jerzy said. Nothing left."

"Then date each one and put them in the packet. And your sketches, Chaim, give them to me."

The printer took the eight sheets of paper Chaim pushed across the table. He then trimmed the excess white edges of each until they were the same size as the photographs. While he cut around their borders, Milutsky stared at the images Chaim had made, the blank stares of the elders before the soldiers arrived — here was Moishe Turkow shielding his face from the fountain's mist or the rabbi pushing his fringed garment deeper into his black trousers — to the unfinished outline, drawn too quickly, of the officer standing in front of Mordcha Rostzat.

Moishe Turkow pulled at the printer's frayed jacket.

"I know, Moishe. I know it's time, but give us a few moments with some brandy before we finish, eh?"

Moishe poured a cup of water over his hands and washed the brown flakes from his lips and cheeks. He took off his holiday hat, crushed on three sides, and ran a wet handkerchief over his dirty forehead.

Milutsky handed Chaim Turkow the thick envelope, opened the seal, and, for the last time, told his apprentice to listen without questioning anything he was about to hear. "There is so little time. I don't have to tell you what you are now holding or what it means — others will do this. But what I —"

The innkeeper raised his voice. "No, Jacob, say 'we.' "

"What *we* are asking is that you leave us and take this with you, this proof of what happened here this afternoon."

The printer took the envelope and wrapped Chaim's hands around the edges. Chaim started to pull away, dropped the packet, and searched for a sign from his father, but Moishe had retreated to the corner, unable to look at either the printer or his apprentice.

"They're in here, my artist — some of the photos we've taken together over the years."

In the fetid darkness of the cellar, made even closer by the odors of sweat and fear and urine, Milutsky still insisted on examining the photographs, and Chaim — Moishe faced the wall — again saw the last few moments of Milutsky's play in the old Zionist Hall: the little girls as blazing comets, whooshing back and forth; his own niece Sorele, dressed as a fern with fronds swaying to her own peculiar music, tripping, one could see, over the dress of the girl next to her; Leybel dangling from the rope that got caught in his beautiful silver wings; and, of course, the Lord perched on his ladder, warning the comets, ferns, and the two lizards (Adam and Meyer Rostzat) to be careful before they fell off the newly made earth.

"Reb Milutsky," Jerzy called from the other side of the cellar's thick door. "Quickly, it's starting to get light outside. Tell him to wear the beret."

But Milutsky was not to be stopped. "Who will remember Sorele or Leybel?" he said, reaching for Chaim's arm. "Don't you understand? Their hair is dark, they have eyes like pieces of charcoal. They won't be able to leave here, Chaim Turkow — and if I believe anything any longer, I believe that officer who told the elders how a fence would be built around the

Jewish section. Today a fence, tomorrow something else. Who knows? Your father can stay inside and hope the days will be short until this terrible business ends. Do I need to hold a mirror in front of your face to show you your own hair and eyes? Did you see that officer today? Did you see his eyes were the same as yours? And could I trust anyone else with this work?"

Jerzy's knocking became more insistent and irritating.

Moishe pulled his son toward the wall. "We have decided: You will take the back road away from here. The Pole will guide you, and since the fence won't be built for a few days, the soldiers, we pray, won't bother someone with golden hair who has a good Polish name and some documents."

"Papa!"

"Not a word. Jacob made these papers for you weeks ago, since he's believed the Germans for eight years. It doesn't matter now if I was an idiot for not listening. It's all arranged: you're now Tadeusz Kazanowski and we've found a place for you to live where you will act the fool again, as you did after the bathhouse. A fool, Chaim, a speechless idiot who remembers nothing of his past. You will work on the estate of a rich Pole suddenly become proud of his good German ancestry, a man Jerzy says who likes blond-haired workers with strong backs. But bathe yourself away from them — some things we cannot change."

"You do this for the sake of these envelopes," Milutsky said when he saw Chaim pulling away from the door. "Don't forget anything, for the sake of the people who saw their children dancing on my stage!"

Jerzy opened the door and motioned for the Jews to come upstairs. They crawled along the shop floor to avoid the reflection from the gas lamp that still illuminated the front room of Milutsky's shop. Chaim gave his coat to Jerzy, put on the one he was given in return. His father helped him button the soiled shirt a fool would undoubtedly wear every day. Moishe Turkow put his hand over his son's mouth. "Go, go, please."

"No more talking," Jerzy said as he opened the front door while holding the bells.

With his father's warm spittle still on his face after a long kiss that had to replace words, Chaim Turkow threw away his Jew's cap, put on Jerzy Fiatkowski's beret, felt Milutsky touch his hand and insert a small piece of charcoal, and obediently followed the Pole to the road leading away from Jacob Schmul Milutsky's shop and the laughing comets of Nowy Dwor.

As a precaution, the two Poles went in a southerly direction before turning northward. Inexperienced in the sounds of war, they couldn't understand the thunderous sounds they heard for eight or nine hours, though no rain ever fell. "Don't turn back," Jerzy warned his friend when the Jew slowed down. "Never turn back when you're a fool."

6

D URING THE FIRST three winters of the war, Witold
Grunewald always treated his handsome fool with
kindness: he allowed him to sleep in an abandoned
pig shelter, gave him permission to eat in the kitchen of the
the estate house after the cooks had finished their own stew,
and — being a loving Christian — insisted that the vacant-
eyed Pole sit outside the Grunewalds' parlor window each
Sunday to listen to the Lutheran hymns Grunewald's wife
played on the newly acquired Austrian piano. For Witold
Grunewald — and the speechless Tadeusz Kazanowski —
there was enough food, little distraction from day-to-day work,
and, with the exception of occasional punitive measures taken
against the peasants by Herr Grunewald's *Kameraden* from
the west, no one suffered or was fearful on the bountiful and
isolated estate.

Like his father and grandfather before him, Herr Grunewald honored and respected his family's beloved ancestral
language and view of the world in this Slavic backwater. But
Herr Grunewald did take pleasure watching this farmhand,
Tadeusz Kazanowski — the only Pole who never gave him any
trouble.

"Look at him," Grunewald would say to his wife when she

put away her music in the oak case. "Have you ever seen a better Polack? He is silent, except for that nice humming he does when you play. He is clean, obedient, and takes good care of the vegetables and pigs!"

The Polish fool (our Chaim Turkow) tending the Grune-wald gardens was the perfect complement to the master's estate. He was blonder than most of the officers who drank Grunewald's wine every Sunday afternoon, he was efficient, and he was incapable of babbling away in the despicable language the family used only when dealing with servants, peasants, or the Polish town authorities. In fact, from the moment this Tadeusz Kazanowski first appeared on the farm during those early hectic days of what Grunewald called "the social reorganization of the Ostland," his entire family praised fate for sending them a servant whose physical beauty was the envy of their neighbors, protectors, and several peasant girls who, though the fool never paid them any attention, occasionally rubbed against his door and left flowers there. And to anyone who asked where this slender, quiet fool came from, Herr Grunewald shrugged his shoulders. "What difference does it make? His papers say he's an orphan who spent his life in institutions. But one look at the fellow will tell you he came from a good Polish mother who had the sense to spread her legs for one of us, I wager! Besides, we take what we can get these days."

In keeping with Herr Grunewald's feelings, therefore, servants in his household and those working on the estate grounds — cooks, maids, laundresses, herdsmen — were instructed to be considerate to the fool who looked so splendid when he carried buckets of steaming manure from the barns or hoed and sprayed the Grunewalds' prize roses. Herr Grunewald reminded all those who sat at his Sunday table how God had seen fit to send them this Tadeusz Kazanowski instead of some filthy gypsy scum. "Such luck only happens," he said, "when a strong will prevails over the land." Trusted by the occupation authorities, many of whose officers sought out his hospitality and his daughter's company, Witold Grunewald was a happy man indeed.

Poland, you see, had been crushed in less than a month by some of the men who now supped with Herr Grunewald and his family. The future was bright, the officers assured them. The new laws enshrining "blood and honor" were in place. The Polacks were terrorized and forbidden to learn more than the alphabet and simple sums. The village's Jews had long ago gone off somewhere. The Bolsheviks would have their balls cut off within the year. And that Yid-sucking, crippled American president would lose heart once the Ukraine turned against Moscow. Witold Grunewald imagined that with a little luck and influence he would soon be called to Krakow as a subminister of agriculture. "Be patient, Witold," the officers told him. "We need people like you." But in nearly two years, Herr Grunewald had never received the long-awaited summons from the Wawel Castle about an appointment; letter after pleading letter went unanswered. Governor-General Hans Frank did not seem to have much time for Witold Grunewald. So Witold told his wife to "let things settle down a bit and warm the bed a little more in the meantime."

As for Tadeusz Kazanowski, who hadn't heard a thunderclap since the day he left Jerzy Fiatkowski, the Grunewald estate offered food, security, and, behind a rotting birch stump fifty meters away from his hut, a hiding place for the photographs and sketches from Nowy Dwor he'd sealed in a large tin that once held a gift of Christmas biscuits from Munich. He learned to live with the stares from the other boys who tended Grunewald's cows and the maids who sometimes let their breasts hang from their blouses when he worked in the barns.

Every night after the Grunewalds and their house servants had said evening prayers and extinguished their lamps, Tadeusz put on his dark wool sweater and, like a parent concerned about a sleeping child, secured his hiding place under the stump with another layer of soil or leaves. He never stayed outside too long, but he always remembered to speak a few words to the images he knew were safely hidden. "So many months now, Papa," he might whisper in Yiddish, or, to the old rabbi who was frozen in black and white next to Pilsudski's monument, "I still say the morning benedictions." Sometimes he told Leybel a story; he even laughed about the comets and lizards. He drew sketches of Manya.

After Tadeusz Kazanowski's third Polish winter finally passed into a muddy, cold spring, Herr Grunewald promised his family and servants they would all celebrate the first pleasant day with a picnic somewhere on the vast estate. "The commandant from the town will also be invited," he told Frau Grunewald, and "we'll make him feel at home with a proper feast, some music, and a little schnapps." Casting a loving glance at his only daughter, Grunewald said he wished, "more than life or honor itself," for her eventual union with one of the commandant's superbly mannered young officers, a pairing he'd be able to arrange given the proper conditions. But when his wife raised a difficult problem — "What German officer wants to marry a girl who was raised in Poland and who knows so little about the Fatherland?" were her exact words — Grunewald laughingly dismissed her concern. "No one has been more for the old ways than we," he shouted in mock anger. "No one respects tradition and good German ways more than we. They know it! I know it!"

Just to be certain, however, that the local commandant did not agree with his wife, Herr Grunewald worked for two weeks on a meticulously researched and illustrated family tree, tracing the ancient limbs and branches of his ancestors back to the original German colonists who settled in certain areas of Poland for the cheap land and, as his own father had once told him, for the "true Protestant way." He omitted the existence of a bastard here and there, and the three Grunewalds a Prussian prince burned at the stake because he thought they were possessed. Witold needed an extra sheet of heavy paper just to show that he, Witold, son of Wolfgang, grandson of Hans, great-grandson of the first Witold, could actually lay claim to being a direct descendant of the Knights Templar. "Men of the Sword and Soil," he wrote under the family's coat-of-arms, changing the original Latin inscription, "Hams from the East to Home," for obvious reasons.

"It's done," he excitedly told Frau Grunewald. "The proof we need: six hundred years of Aryan manhood." As luck would have it, the sun finally came out under a glorious blue sky just as the ink dried on the spectacular history of the family Grunewald.

Fräulein Grunewald was given leave to order a new dress from Warsaw and the picnic was set for the following Saturday, a celebration to be noted in the gardener's hut by Chaim Turkow as the one hundred seventieth Shabbos he'd spent away from Nowy Dwor.

✦ ✦ ✦

Herr and Frau Grunewald made elaborate preparations. Not only would this first grand picnic of the year be a stage upon which to display their only daughter and dead relatives, but it would also help their brother knights celebrate the intoxicating victory of arms. Herr Grunewald made an inventory of his best wines, ordered sausages from his smokehouses, sent precise orders to his kitchens for pastries and the dark, rich bread he wanted prepared in the Bavarian style. Using a picture taken from the album of her engagement party, Frau Grunewald showed Tadeusz Kazanowski the varieties of colorful flowers he should pick from the garden for the picnic tables.

"And my camera equipment, too," Herr Grunewald instructed the Polish fool in the hated language of his adopted land. "Your job is to hold the camera when I am with my guests." Although Chaim nodded his head to show he understood his master, he could hardly keep his legs from buckling at Grunewald's mention of the camera. "You're right to feel anxious," Grunewald said when he noticed the fool's cheeks lose all color. "Who wouldn't be nervous at the thought of such a splendid festivity?"

On the chosen Saturday, everything was prepared long before the guests arrived at the estate. Tadeusz Kazanowski was allowed thirty minutes to wash himself and dress in his cleanest peasant shirt. "Something simple," Frau Grunewald requested, with her eye for detail and local custom. "Our officers do enjoy seeing the folk colors you people love. Herr Grunewald might also ask you to hum one of our beautiful hymns, so I want you to be a bright star for all of us."

Tadeusz returned to his hut to scrape the cow droppings from his boots. Halfway between the hut and the barns, he caught his first glimpse of some pigs running and snorting along the path he used to reach the buried biscuit tin. Some of the animals carried half-eaten bits of garbage; others were screaming with their snouts upturned and blue from rooting in the cook's wild-berry patch. Picking up a stick to beat the animals back to their pens, Tadeusz managed to catch up with the slower sows and frighten all but one into a full retreat. "Ay, away," he shouted when he saw her chewing something she'd pulled from a deep hole by the stump. "Ayyy!" When the animal saw him coming too close, she ran directly toward Tadeusz, lowered her filthy head, and bit into his leg above the right ankle. The pig returned to the stump and took hold of a few bitter roots attached to a nearby stump.

Tadeusz came closer to the pig, and since he was too frightened to yell again, he smashed the stick into the pig's rump. The animal made one final plunge into the soft ground on the opposite side of the stump, chewing on what fell out of a sweet-smelling tin. Once again Tadeusz struck out at the animal's hairy rump — a blow that made the pig snort, then back away from the stump — but not before it vomited a wet mound of leaves and paper. Chaim Turkow fell into the sticky mess, and after pulling the pulp apart, he found the pig had destroyed all but two of the photographs and one sketch that had stuck to the bottom of the tin.

"Praise be to Christ," Elzbieta, the Grunewalds' old cook, called over and over. "Where are you, Tadek?"

The sunlight shone on the worn path Chaim had followed to the pig's last stand. Pig droppings and spots of blood — from the boy and the animal — glistened on the large oak leaves along the ground.

"Answer, Tadek," she called. "The officers have arrived and they want you to serve. Where are you?"

Chaim took the two surviving photographs and the one remaining sketch from the crushed tin and stuffed them inside his blouse. When the old woman found him he'd already thrown the pulpy remnants of the destroyed photos and sketches into the pig's hole, and though any movement made his lacerated leg burn, he covered the hole with dirt and packed it down with his boots.

"Why are you jumping up and down on shit?" Elzbieta asked her master's fool. "Don't you know the Kraut-lovers want to show you off? Didn't you hear me?"

✦   ✦   ✦

Under a clear blue sky, Herr Grunewald watched his wonderful guests enjoying the old-style food piled high on his wife's best Limoges dishes, the chilled wine in earthenware pitchers, and the songs he coaxed Frau Grunewald into playing on the small piano his Polack dairyman pulled to the picnic ground in his cart. Even during the war, he thought to himself as he watched the officers devouring his sausages and schnapps, we're all brothers.

Grunewald's daughter was the perfect hostess, too. She fretted over the smallest details, refilling glasses with her father's choicest wines while openly flirting with a particularly handsome lieutenant who clapped when Frau Grunewald began to play his favorite marches on the well-tuned piano. After a few glasses of wine, Fräulein Grunewald took little notice of the slightly intoxicated young officer's hand playing over her ruffled Warsaw dress.

"Yes, Fräulein," he was overhead saying after finishing a spicy sausage. "They have all been gathered in a few places. Who would ever have thought it would work so smoothly?" After another bottle of wine the lieutenant told her he had "high hopes of being promoted" as soon as his "special unit moved further east," but he stopped short of explaining the unique nature of his duties in the field (especially those dealing with difficult operations later perfected by the sides of freshly excavated pits in the Ukraine) when his captain cast a disapproving glance toward him. "Forget such boring business, Joachim. Today we are here with friends!" It was time, the lieutenant knew, to shut his mouth.

The Grunewalds' Polish servants stayed in their assigned places by the tables. Only Tadeusz Kazanowski received permission to remain next to several beautiful horses the officers planned to ride when the conversation stagnated. He held Herr Grunewald's camera and waited, even though his leg throbbed and the salve Elzbieta had applied burned and smarted. The fool stared at the gelding's shiny haunches and mumbled something Herr Grunewald was too far away to hear.

On cue (everything had been rehearsed for days), Frau Grunewald stopped playing. "So tell us, Witold," she said gaily, "how can we best remember this special day with our friends?"

Witold Grunewald smiled, paused as if he were considering the possibilities, and raised his hands toward his assembled company, "By photographs, my love," he answered, to the applause of his daughter and the muffled groans of the lieutenant. "We should look our best for the future, for history, eh, Herr Major?" When the major smiled, Herr Grunewald beckoned the young man guarding the horses. "The camera, Tadeusz," he ordered. "Bring me my memory box!"

Chaim tried to conceal his hobbling gait. Shu, sha, baby, he thought, remembering the words of the lullaby his mother sang when he had such terrible dreams as a child. Shu (right foot) . . . sha (left foot) . . . baby. . . . Papa . . . never . . . sleeps.

"Come, everyone, now I've got it. Everyone stand by the big tree while we still have this good light."

Frau Grunewald joined the seven officers and her daughter. While her husband attached the expensive camera to a wooden tripod and busied himself looking for just the right angle, the officers continued to drink and laugh. Every so often, as befitted an occasion turning melancholy because of schnapps, wine, and homesickness, they told one another how they missed their own families, who must, it was generally agreed, be enjoying equally splendid weather in the Reich.

Herr Grunewald wrapped a thin black shutter cord around his left hand. "Ready, gentlemen. Please, now, quiet. Wear your most contented expressions as I count to three."

With the major calling for silence, his brother officers pulled their tunics into their belts. To a man, they made one pass with their sleeves over the shiny silver insignia that noted their special status. When he pressed his eye next to the camera viewfinder, Witold Grunewald was pleased to note how brightly the death's-head emblem on their uniforms reflected the sunlight.

"Eins, zwei, drei, boom," said the descendant of so many noble ancestors. "Boom!"

Herr Grunewald was like a sturdy locomotive, moving back and forth in front of the officers, taking one snap after another at various angles. He made his wife and daughter stand by each of the officers in turn ("Eins, zwei, drei, boom!"), and several officers made special requests to be photographed next to the horses or with the Grunewald servant girls sitting on their laps. The major, however, was growing bored and tired of the grotesque obsequiousness of the *Volksdeutscher*. "Enough, Grunewald," he finally said. "More music from the Frau and no more 'booms.'" Obliging to a fault, Witold stepped away from the camera, only to have the major apologize for being so abrupt. "This day would never have been possible without you," the major added. "Why not become a part of a few photographs yourself? Come, Grunewald, do join us."

"But who will make our photograph, Herr Major?"

The major was quite used to making decisions on the spot. "That Pole over there," he said, pointing to Tadeusz. "Give him the camera, Grunewald."

Chaim listened to Herr Grunewald's hurried instructions. "Your hand must go over here," he said, placing the Pole's sweaty fingers on the brushed metal. "Not over the lens, but right on the shutter snap. Wait for the shadows to pass and hold your breath, and don't kick the tripod." Tadeusz nodded. Herr Grunewald found a place to stand between Frau Grunewald and the major. The sun was momentarily concealed by a huge white cloud. "Wait, Tadeusz," Herr Grunewald yelled from his honored position on the major's right side. "Be patient and wait for more light."

Through the small glass viewfinder that framed the upsidedown officers and the Grunewalds, Chaim Turkow studied the happy group. A subaltern passed a bottle of wine from hand to hand to relieve the monotonous waiting. The lieutenant called Joachim was very close to Fräulein Grunewald and held her hand next to his trousers; the elder Grunewalds toasted the honor of the major's unit, and soon all began to sing a slow, sad song they usually enjoyed after their work in the fields and forests was finished for the day. Chaim waited, since he knew the precise moment when the precious light would reveal natural expressions and the best details.

"It's time," someone shouted. "God knows it's time for the picture!"

The fool did his counting by waving once, twice, three times. In all: fifteen waves made for the five photographs Tadeusz clicked off with skill. Herr Grunewald was quick to note that the fool never moved the camera or let out his breath.

"Bravo!" the officers cried. "More music, there's been enough documentation for one day."

With the exception of the sound made by the wind blowing through the leaves, and Fräulein Grunewald's giggling when the lieutenant's hand found a soft spot under her Warsaw dress, all was quiet until Frau Grunewald struck the opening note of one of her husband's favorite hymns. Herr Grunewald sobbed with joy as his wife played.

Soon after Frau Grunewald struck the last slightly-off-key chord, the captain rushed to congratulate the *Volksdeutscher*'s wife. The major however, excused himself and walked away from the Grunewalds to where the fool stood with the camera. The captain quickly joined his commandant with a new bottle and a fresh packet of cigarettes. Perhaps it was the music that made the major feel in the mood to talk about something he'd seen only a few weeks before in a forest much like the one bordering the *Volksdeutscher*'s pleasant estate.

"Do you remember that old Jew who was with his brothers by the pit, Richard?" he said to the captain. "He was naked and shivering, and he was standing next to this child, a little girl, I think. 'Please, sir,' he asked me, 'can I do a trick for the baby?' 'Go ahead,' I said, 'let's see what you can do.' So then he takes five stones from the ground, does some sort of twisting with his wrists, and juggles all of them for at least two minutes. The kid stops crying as soon as the old man mumbles something and gets one of the stones to appear in her hair. Amazing, I've never seen anything like it before, even in Hamburg. I'm still thinking how much my nephews would like to see this when I go home to visit them on leave."

The major, a bit tipsy from the Grunewalds' good wine, imitated the Jew trying to keep his balance at the edge of the pit, including the way he stroked the child and pointed up toward the sky.

"I'm yelling — yelling, mind you — at the Yid. 'What's the trick? Come on, what have you got to lose by telling me?' and when I went to take a quick piss, some damn impatient ass behind me thinks he now has permission to give the order. Now I've never done this before, but I made the corporal wait before he threw the quicklime over the bodies. Maybe, I thought, the old man is still wiggling around and could tell me about the trick. No luck, though . . . Still, that Yid had a gift — to be able to make five stones fly up and down like that! It was amazing, I tell you, and now it's all gone."

✦ ✦ ✦

That night, feasting on leftovers too good for the slop pail, Elzbieta would tell the other maids how she came upon young Tadek after his pig hunt and how the pretty one was making these strange noises even as she helped him to his feet. "It almost sounded like a Jew-chant, like the ones I used to hear when the Jews walked to their cemetery in town."

"God protect us from such stuff," one of the other maids answered, spitting on the ground to ward off the evil eye responsible for such a thought. "I dare you to say that to Father Grabowski after mass!"

At the same time that old Elzbieta was telling the other Polish women about the funny tune Tadek hummed all the way to the house, Chaim was in his hut, studying the photographs and the sketch of his sisters he'd saved from the animal.

One of the photos taken by Milutsky before the soldiers drove into the square with their flag and the Rostzat sons, showed nine unsuspecting elders by the fountain, all wearing such good hats and clean suits. Moishe Turkow had his head turned away from Jacob's lens. Perhaps he'd heard and engine's roar echoing over his shoulder. This photograph had a crease across the top and a slight tear that ran in a jagged line halfway across the rabbi's face.

Chaim put the second, and last, photo next to the first. Slowly turning it toward the candle, he studied each detail of Leybel's silver wings, his curled earlocks, the rope that held the boy suspended above Milutsky's paper world and Nowy Dwor. He looked at the boy's smile as he flew between the rocks, "I tried, Papa," Chaim said. "I tried to keep them safe."

This is what the former apprentice of Jacob Schmul Milutsky did then: he broke the law by saying a Kaddish for the lost faces of Nowy Dwor, knowing, as he did, that this holiest of prayers required the presence of at least ten Jewish men. What would the rabbi have said if he learned how Chaim Turkow, swaying in the corner of a sty, decided that, including himself along with the nine stationary elders still fixed in position on a torn photograph, the number ten had been reached? It's a difficult question, isn't it?

Safe in his solitary minyan, Chaim later tried to sketch a

half-remembered face on a sheet of newspaper, once-skilled fingers shading and rubbing lines with Milutsky's gift of charcoal until he, Chaim Turkow, had almost turned his father's face around. All the while, he paid no attention to the loud music coming from the house, the cheers, or the racket made by the drunken officers smashing wineglasses against Herr Grunewald's front steps. And this, too: after forgetting how the crease in his father's broad forehead stretched the full width of the innkeeper's brow before it was bisected by a pinkish scar (a deep line he and Manya used to touch with their children's fingers), Chaim Turkow could draw only the simplest figures — a few squares, a three-dimensional box, and what seemed to be a circle.

"Shu . . . sha . . . shu . . . sha . . ."

7

I N T H E Y E A R S since Chaim Turkow had become Tadeusz
Kazanowski, he never left the Grunewald estate. He lived
within the small area in which Witold Grunewald allowed
him freedom: the dairy barn, a small garden plot, his wooden
hut, Elzbieta's kitchen and smokehouse. As a fool without
words, Tadeusz Kazanowski was a harmless enough creature,
requiring minimal care and notice; Chaim Turkow, however,
tried to keep what was left of his promise by covering his head,
praying whenever he could, and working on his charcoal
sketches every night. And it was during the month when the
snow piled high in huge drifts against his hut — the same
snow, it was said by the Polish peasants, that was making the
corporal's finest troops eat the livers of their slain brothers
close to Stalingrad — that Chaim Turkow forgot his own age
and the color of Manya's eyes. The year of his birth slipped
away from him just as the sketches from Nowy Dwor began
to crumble at the edges in brittle, yellow pieces. He was, we
should say, too tired to care, even if he wasn't sure of the first
Hebrew word of the Shema prayer. "Is it 'Here' or 'Hear'?" he
asked himself. No answer came.

However, sometime during Chaim Turkow's fourth winter
away from Nowy Dwor, the Grunewald household began to

change: the servants were no longer invited to listen to Frau Grunewald's thirty-minute recitals on Sundays; Chaim was never asked to contribute his choral humming to the worship service; and Fräulein Grunewald, still unmarried, was rarely seen outside her bedroom door after that frosty morning when she learned of her young Joachim's valiant death close to the Soviet border. For Witold Grunewald, now regularly dining on fatty soup with the occasional piece of sausage floating in the bowl, the days revolved around listening to the buzzing and crackling sounds that came from his wireless set — tuned from morning to night to the official war news — and studying the oversized maps of Europe he pinned to his study walls.

Gone, too, were those happy moments when the officers in the crisp uniforms would sing and recite their adventures to the Grunewalds. Almost all of them had been sent to help over-burdened comrades elsewhere, to places, Herr Grunewald suspected, where they would be very busy for some time. But just to be sure he knew everything, Herr Grunewald listened to every hourly broadcast. He even let the fool come into his study to hear an especially good bit of news while Elzbieta's food remained uneaten on the tray she set beside her master's door.

"It's the war that's doing it," Elzbieta reported to the other maids and Tadeusz Kazanowski. "The old man sits in front of those maps and sticks pins into the brown parts. I say to him, 'Pan Grunewald, take some tea, please,' and all he does is yell at me or throw his shoe at the wireless. Well, it's not the food, I can tell you. Not my food!"

Left alone at night in his freezing hut, Chaim worked by candlelight. He still tended the two emaciated dairy cows that were left on the estate, pulling their sorry teats for a dribble of sour-smelling milk. He chopped wood for Elzbieta's stove and carried sacks of grain from the estate's dwindling stores. He ate his meals without expression (though he learned to bless each meal while pretending to scratch his head). On those special feast days when he was asked to come into the warm kitchen with the other servants, Elzbieta liked to read to him from the Bible or the lives of the holy saints. But she never understood why he kept his beret on.

"Bad vapors get caught in the forehead," she teased, tugging at the beret. "Let them out and you might even get your voice back." Of course, Tadeusz Kazanowski learned to make the sign of the cross just like the peasant women who washed the Grunewalds' clothes or emptied slops into the pigpens. And Tadek learned to show his love of Christ by crying at the appropriate moment during the life of a certain Catholic martyr. Seeing how moved the fool was during such moments, Elzbieta gave him candles, incense, and a miniature portrait of the Black Madonna for the shrine in his hut. "You say your beads every day and light a candle," she urged the fool. "Praise be to Christ, lost one."

"And may He save our Poland!" the laundress added. The other maids lowered their heads and voices. "Poland," they said in unison. "Poland forever."

A loyal daughter of the One True Church, Elzbieta knew Poland would survive, but the state of her immortal soul was of more importance — even during a war that sucked the village's boys away from home and brought the Antichrist to the countryside. And so the old cook would let the girls have their say, their "Poland forever" cries with wet eyes showing their feeling, and then proceed, by virtue of her spiritual and temporal seniority, to hit each one of them with a strap. "It's Christ above all," she yelled. "Don't you ever forget!" Tadek, however, was never slapped or touched in any way. "Because the Lord Jesus is in his soul," the cook said to a weeping girl. "Such emptiness in the brain must mean something."

But then there was Herr Grunewald's need to talk about the war in the east. Alone day after day in his study, without the comfort of his wife, daughter, or the officers who once told him everything, Witold Grunewald listened to the wireless reports and moved little pins around on his large military field map. In one breathless, jubilant message after another, the official voice of Berlin noted the tremendous changes in Europe's geography, the routing of armies in the face of Teutonic power. Herr Grunewald always poured himself a few large tumblers of brandy as soon as the Party's anthem reached its climax, calling out in German to his empty room, "Mark the path of glory, time for the pins to move!"

Witold Grunewald faced his precious map: Red pins for the Panzer divisions in their gallant eastward roll through the homeland of the Jewish-Bolshevik vermin. Blue pins closing in on Moscow, grazing the suburbs of Stalingrad and Peter's great city on the Neva. Black pins encircling Warsaw, Lodz, Krakow, all of the Ukraine.

Each time the Berlin announcer spoke about the New Order, Herr Grunewald moved his blue and red pins (the black-ribboned one, of course, stayed in place as a small but permanent shrine to Joachim). But who would share the news with him? Who, after all, would be capable of listening to the master of the house speak about such blessed times? Frau Grunewald spent her days trying to coax Fräulein Grunewald from her room. "A lost cause and a cold bed," Witold mumbled, and then added an ancient family obscenity. Moreover, he knew the Poles who still brought him his food were worthless louts who hated his language and his sympathies for the conqueror. "And what's worse," he once yelled so loud that Elzbieta heard him in the kitchen, "is that I can't even get on top of her with all these Polacks around me!"

Naturally, this is why Herr Witold Grunewald continued to drink until, on the very day he felt Stalingrad was at last about to surrender (though it fell the other way, taking von Paulus's hundred divisions deeper into one another and the Russian winter), Tadeusz Kazanowski accidentally cut himself with the shovel he was using to clear the ice from the path below Herr Grunewald's study window.

"How is he?" the master asked Elzbieta when he saw her crouching next to the brilliantly stained snow. "Is it serious?"

"No, Pan Grunewald," the old woman answered. "He'll be back at his work in a few minutes. Just needs a little bandage to stop the red stuff."

He watched his maid wrap the boy's leg, pat him on his head, and point to the shovel. She's telling him to go back to work, Herr Grunewald thought, and the fool never complains or even hums a protest! What a tragedy that someone with such blood and nerve had to be an idiot in the asshole of central Europe.

"Tadeusz Kazanowski," Herr Grunewald found himself saying through the blast of cold wind that rushed through the window into his overheated room. "Put that damn shovel down and come inside for a moment. Sit by my fire until the wind dies off." A humane man, Witold Grunewald was also sensible: one is never, he well knew, unkind to productive farm animals or compliant Slavs.

Tadeusz Kazanowski entered the room and bowed, his clumsy feet uncomfortable in the pool of water created by the quickly melting snow from Herr Grunewald's land. As was customary in such circumstances, he removed his cap (a necessity for Tadeusz; an act requiring a plea for God's understanding from Chaim). "Sit down, Tadek," he heard. "The old woman will clean everything up."

Despite the pain of his wound, Tadeusz still wiped his boots with his coat sleeve and sat on the edge of Herr Grunewald's massive leather chair. The fire glowed and spat tiny sparks that hovered above the logs for a second before floating up into the stone chimney. Herr Grunewald gave the fool a glass of vodka without looking at him or asking after his welfare: he had, we're certain, more important things to consider.

"Drink up, boy," Herr Grunewald said. "It's time for the afternoon broadcast." Drawing another leather chair close to the wireless — its oversized oak case dominated an entire corner of the comfortable room — Tadek's thoughful employer turned the polished radio toward his guest. A few adjustments of the black knobs brought the first sounds from Berlin. Herr Grunewald rose in front of the wireless and directed his Pole to do likewise. "Up, up," he said, motioning with his hands (he thought it appropriate to speak to the blue-eyed Pole in German — a first lesson in the mother tongue) as he counted the five seconds it would take until the anthem began with a long drumroll.

Side by side, this audience of two listened to the guttural shrieks that made the pins vibrate along the Danube.

"Do you understand what he's saying, Tadek?"

Tadeusz shrugged and looked at the floor, though he remained at mock-attention throughout the music and the noise that followed; Chaim Turkow understood almost every word, the transition from Yiddish to German an easy step.

"Victories everywhere," Herr Grunewald shouted, "from Kiev to Moscow. Tens of thousands greeting our armies with outstretched arms and . . ."

"Advances" was a better translation of Herr Grunewald's first word in the sentence, Chaim thought. From Kiev to Moscow, the army *advances*.

". . . there is a need for faith in the eventual victory over the Jew menace."

Chaim's back tightened. He stroked his capless head. Yes, *Juden. Juden.* Same word!

"Thanks be to God," Herr Grunewald said when the speaker finished his pointed report.

Chaim nodded. Same word: *Gott.*

"Now for the pins," Herr Grunewald said to the Pole, who hardly knew where to stand or what to do. "We go to the map and mark another day's progress."

Witold Grunewald saluted the wireless, grabbed the bottle of brandy and the little box he kept next to the speaker, and joyously began moving red pins to the right, eastward — every move in accordance with the truth he'd just heard form Berlin. Tadeusz Kazanowski stood beside him while he explained the intricacies of strategic maneuvers taking place beyond the Vistula.

"The plan is so simple!" Herr Grunewald waved his hands and pointed to one place after another on the map. "The army moves, overwhelms resistance, reestablishes civil order. Look at all of these pins, Tadek!"

In his euphoric state, Herr Grunewald ignored Elzbieta's knocking on the study door. Who needed a slice or two of green sausage with black bread when there was so much to explain?

But as his hand finally rested along a mountain range in the interior of another subjugated country, Herr Grunewald stole a quick glance at the Polish fool and realized that he, Witold Grunewald, had all the while been reinventing the world in German without bothering to translate anything for the benefit of his sober and stupid companion.

"*Mein Gott*, now we have to begin all over again." He shouted at Elzbieta (the old woman never gave up her knocking): "Go away with those slops, you sow!" And equally loudly to Tadeusz Kazanowski: "Button your coat, have another drink. We're going outside to the war!"

Herr Grunewald put on his long coat with the fox collar and remembered to take his favorite riding crop. He poured, and then drank, two large glasses of brandy. His inner strength fortified by the strong, amber-colored liquid, he rummaged through some papers on his desk until he found a smaller version of the map that adorned his wall.

Herr Grunewald flung open the door and announced his intentions in Polish. "To the snow, Tadeusz Kazanowski. What you can't understand in words will now be demonstrated through actions." Herr Grunewald neither apologized to nor even took note of the old woman who lay sprawled on his polished floor in a mess of greasy sausage and cabbage soup.

Witold Grunewald, the self-proclaimed Knight Templar, marched past the old Polish woman. As soon as he was outside with his fool next to him, he began to march and sing through the snowdrifts.

To Herr Grunewald, the matter at hand was entirely serious, far beyond the understanding of the red Polack faces peering at him through frosted windows. He ordered Tadeusz to gather sixteen logs from the woodpile, a basket of stones from the shed, and several long branches from the dead birch tree. And while his servant made ready the armaments necessary to carry out his plan, Herr Grunewald perched atop a large stump that provided a perfect spot from which to survey his map and battlefield.

The wind became stronger.

"Five logs in a line, like so," Herr Grunewald told the Pole, marking out a line with one of the birch branches. "Ten over here." Checking his map to get the exact scale he knew was important, Herr Grunewald instructed Tadeusz to drop the black stones on top of the curving trail he gouged out with his riding crop from one end of the garden to the other. "Now we have Poland," he said when the borders were drawn to his satisfaction over an area covering about thirty square meters. "The Bolshies are next."

More stones, more logs, more carefully outlined borders etched with the branch. The stones were cities, the logs triumphant German divisions. Herr Grunewald with his map stood in the middle of it all. "The *Führer* in Berlin," he yelled, "couldn't have a better view of things."

In the hour they spent together in the Polish snow, Herr Grunewald and his faithful adjutant rolled logs over the cities named by the *Führer* himself as "festering sores on the world's body." Starting from the stone that became Warsaw (soon kicked aside by Herr Grunewald as a worthless impediment), they pushed and shoved their divisions to within a few kilometers of the border where the brave soldiers who once graced Herr Grunewald's estate were probably serving, and dying, for the Fatherland. If the fool seemed puzzled by a maneuver,

Herr Grunewald would snap his crop and demonstrate how an army moves over the rail lines and muddied roads of barbaric countries. Herr Grunewald kicked Tadeusz and told him to push some logs northward into Byelorussia, toward Minsk. "Here is our real battle," he said when he crossed the Polish-Soviet border. "Hurry, pick up some of those stones and dribble them close to Moscow. Bomb the hell out of them. The Ostland, you idiot," Grunewald was saying as he waved his crop and bottle. "Have another drink."

"Freeze away your soul, devil," Elzbieta said to no one in particular from her kitchen window. "Stay out there long enough and maybe your tube will crack off!"

Tadeusz followed every order Herr Grunewald gave in his mixture of Polish and German. "We move with a strong will," Herr Grunewald screamed as the wind became louder and the snow began to blow across the expanding field of battle. "The world is ours." And to prove his point, he danced from one conquered country to another: a heel digging into Moscow, a toe sliding over the Crimea. He didn't seem to notice that his beautiful coat was now open or that tiny icicles had already begun to hang from his exposed shirt.

When there were no more cities left, when all the major roads were under the authority of the *Führer*'s log divisions, Witold Grunewald turned to his servant, hoping that the blue-eyed, blond fool would finally be able to draw upon the mystical power that must be resident in anyone with such obviously Aryan features.

"Applaud, young Tadek," Herr Grunewald yelled. "Show me you understand."

Tadeusz Kazanowski scraped the frozen drool from his chin and stared at the white ground. He pulled at his crotch and picked his nose. Once, he winced from the shooting pain that spread down his leg, and though he didn't wish it to happen, he had to run over to the *Führer*'s former birch stump, where he pissed a long, hot stream over Berlin.

"I see this is nothing more than a game to you," said the field marshal in response to the Pole's idiotic act. "Such a waste. Get the snot off your face, Polack. Go to the barn and ready the sleigh for a trip to town. Your day will not end *until you understand!*"

Herr Grunewald took a drink from his silver flask to prepare himself for the long ride. He looked at the battlefield and the drops of blood, at the yellow crater where Berlin had fallen. He walked over to the high ground between Poland and the Soviet Union, backed up to Warsaw, and, weather-veteran that he was who needed revenge, dropped his thick trousers and defecated on Poland's capital. When he was finished, Herr Grunewald saw a curtain in his kitchen move and a hand clear away a patch of frost.

"Hey, old bitch," he yelled when he saw Elzbieta. "Open that damn window and listen. Pack some food for my trip to Modlin with the idiot — and be sure to put in extra measures of sausage and brandy. Put my camera on top so I can bring back a snap or two to show all of you. *Can you hear me, Pani Polack?* I'm going to show our little Tadek here how we've fucked them up the ass!"

He ran over the entire snow map with its quickly disappearing borders, then attempted to jump onto the sleigh's runner, lost his footing, and tried again. Elzbieta hurried out and threw a large sack into the sleigh. She spat, three times, behind the field marshal's wide rump.

Herr Grunewald hoisted himself into the sleigh and

motioned for the fool to sit down. With the poise of a great officer, he rose and waved to the old woman, who watched as the sleigh made a wide turn around his yard over the stones that must have been Krakow or Lublin.

8

I MAGINE THIS SIGHT: Herr Grunewald bundled beneath a fur coverlet, his face warmed by the fox collar of his coat and the heat of his brandy, barely able to control the angry horse that had no wish to pull the loaded sleigh over the slippery road; Tadeusz Kazanowski's head covered by a blanket like a peasant on his way to market. For Witold Grunewald, the first trip to town in three weeks; for Tadeusz Kazanowski, the only trip he'd ever been allowed away from his hut, the dairy cows, and Elzbieta's kitchen. "Don't be afraid, Polack," Herr Grunewald said to the fool next to him. "Proof is coming!"

Next: the arrival in Modlin as the afternoon light began to grow pink and blue over the Church of the Holy Mother. Herr Grunewald's hands were closed around the leather reins, but when he saw the military vehicles, he poked the fool and pointed to the German flag over the railroad station. The horse's flanks steamed when the sleigh passed soldiers huddled next to open fires. Tadek's master threw out a bottle of schnapps and some German greetings to them.

The station was filled with uniformed men who looked as if they'd just been given a short break from a tedious job. Non-commissioned officers shared cigarettes with their men; eight or nine Polish policemen kept to themselves, talking quietly; a squad of SS soldiers avoided everyone except their own officer, who, even in the freezing wind, was counting the cattlecars that were being shunted into the back of the railyard by a small locomotive.

Witold Grunewald found his best reception among the regular Wehrmacht soldiers.

"Your German is perfect," a tired officer told him. "Better than mine."

"Then have a packet of cigarettes," the *Volksdeutscher* replied to this gracious compliment, "and suck in the sweet aroma from Hamburg's best smoke."

The soldiers toasted Herr Grunewald with his own schnapps while their officer (he now held two packets of cigarettes) told Witold that, yes, he could stay awhile at the station. "But just keep away from those rear platforms." None of the soldiers paid any attention to the shivering Polack behind the happy Herr Grunewald.

"Will you allow me to take a few snaps of your men, sir?" Witold asked. "My wife and daughter need a bit of cheering up — and if they could see these trains!"

"No trains, *mein Herr*," snapped the officer. "My men, yes — but no pictures of the trains."

"Come along, you," Herr Grunewald said to Tadeusz, loudly enough to show the officer exactly how to manage a Pole. "Permission has been granted."

In the time it took a very excited photographer to arrange the soldiers and the officer in the proper way in front of his camera, he also counted the seventeen cattlecars that shrieked over the cold tracks. A bottle of schnapps — this one offered by the officer to Herr Grunewald — meant that an entire roll of film would be shot. What's more important, Herr Grunewald would learn something about the nature of this busy station's work from an officer who would gladly talk to a fellow German in a language spiced with expressions one often heard in cabarets or drinking cellars.

"Pay no mind to the Polack," said Herr Grunewald. "He doesn't understand German or anything else."

The officer, weaving slightly from the strong drink taken on an empty stomach, explained how the "items" passed through the Modlin depot.

"Easier than moving horses, my friend. We're now moving almost two thousand every day. They don't have to be fed, their brats take up almost no space at all in the cars, and we even get them to pay us for the trip!"

The officer's words nearly took Herr Grunewald's breath away. He stared open-mouthed at the cattlecars moving behind a high fence at the side of the station.

"Two thousand per day — I never thought it possible!"

"Up from fifteen hundred. Not bad, eh?"

"Why, sir, you *must* accept my congratulations."

"We've reamed them out from the eastern provinces, and now we begin working the larger cities. You have my word: the shit will be cleaned up as fast as we can shovel it aboard!"

Such bragging earned the officer three smoked sausages from Herr Grunewald's hamper. Several trains began to pull away from the platform in a swirl of steam and shooting cinders. The officer saw Grunewald's fool watching the black coats alight onto the few passenger coaches coupled to the end of a long train of cattlecars. "Horses," the officer said to Tadeusz in broken Polish. "German soldiers need lots of horses."

Herr Grunewald repeated the officer's numbers as a sign of

respect, and, as if he had to confirm such startling information, he pumped the hand of his informant and then bowed. "Please, you must let me offer my best to your brothers," he said, pointing to the rear platform. "If for no other reason than to distribute a few gifts." He turned to the fool. "Tadek, go and bring my special hamper," he ordered the Pole. "Hurry, now, there isn't much time."

Chaim returned to the sleigh and lifted the heavy wicker basket, which was still fragrant with the aroma of Elzbieta's sweet sausage and meat pies. But when he returned, he found a young SS soldier waiting for the promised gifts.

"Your master says to wait for him here," the soldier said in halting Polish as he uncovered the basket and saw the Grunewald offering. But then he took pity on the fool, who stood shivering and stupid in the wind, and told him to stand under a tin shelter close to some luggage. "Go on, no one will bother you."

The afternoon light was fast disappearing, and the trains blew billows of steam everywhere. Head lowered — he was now close to the kind of men who had driven into the market square in Nowy Dwor — Chaim Turkow found an open corner under the sagging metal shelter. Although he could hear the trains moving and the Germans shouting orders on the other side of the shelter's wall, he could see almost nothing of the railyard because of the hundreds of piled crates and valises surrounding the shelter. But he did see, not far away, the end of a train backing along a rail siding: it moved slowly and deliberately, loaded with a cargo that occasionally slammed against the cars' wooden walls.

Chaim crouched in the corner of the shelter. He was grateful for the warm steam that drifted from the trains over to where he now sat waiting for Herr Grunewald. Gradually all the noises — the screeching of metal wheels on frozen tracks, the muffled knocking against wooden cattlecar walls, the Germans' orders to their dogs — grew louder. As he rested against his corner, a valise close to Chaim shifted slightly, giving him a narrow view of the activity that Witold Grunewald, sitting fifty meters away in a warm building and drinking the dregs of his cherry brandy with an amiable black-coated officer, promised not to reveal to anyone. Naturally, with five or six bottles left and the sweet sausages still left to be shared among the group surrounding Herr Grunewald, not much attention was being paid to the obedient shuffling outside of a few thousand "items" they all knew were moving because of a stroke of organizational genius. Certainly, the officers and Herr Grunewald soon forgot about the idiot under the shelter.

What is it possible to see between two leather valises? What moves through such a confined field of vision, no wider that a thin wedge of poor man's cheese? Some sections of railcars (they were cattlecars with metal ties across the doors) with illegible chalk markings? Or maybe a Polish engineer halting his oily locomotive so he can have a chat with the station-master? A few dogs straining at their leashes? The surname on the edge of a handbag that hangs from a corner of one of those valises?

It doesn't matter, for only moments before Witold Grune-wald, sour-smelling before his collapse, staggered into the fresh air, Chaim Turkow saw this: a stick of an arm, thin as a ragdoll's, moving up and down through a broken slat in an otherwise secure cattlecar. Chaim pushed his eye to the opening between the valises and saw the arm move and wave until a face (was it the ragdoll's?) took its place. Then the train jerked backward, and the face vanished from Chaim Turkow's frame. After a screeching of wheels, the train lurched forward again. That face (boy? girl?) returned, seemed to notice the wall of luggage and handbags, and shouted a name that was lost in all of the other noises.

Chaim kept his eye next to the opening, his sliver of darkening afternoon. As the train moved slowly forward, he counted seventy more arms hanging from cattlecars. He also saw a red babushka, a hand, and, just as his eye began to tear from the cold wind, the long hair of a woman that had somehow been caught between two slats in the cattlecar's wall. A soldier with a dog finally blocked Chaim's sight, the animal leaving a turd, the soldier a can of disinfectant. Seventy arms, Chaim Turkow said to himself. And one babushka. (But who knows? The eye — only one was used here, mind you — plays tricks in cold weather, maybe the same kind of trick that once made Moishe Turkow believe in the miraculous curative power of the Narew.)

"Time to pick up your master," the officer finally called to Tadeusz after the last train had passed through the station. "The good man has fainted away from us."

After many hours of drinking and singing with the wet-eyed *Volksdeutscher*, the uniforms had to let their benefactor go home. Tadeusz Kazanowski bore the dead weight of Witold Grunewald all the way from the stationhouse to the sleigh. Herr Grunewald revived in his seat when, following an officer's instructions, the fool rubbed some snow over Witold's face.

Once revived, Herr Grunewald began to sing the lyric the officer's men so enjoyed during their time together. "And she jumped on his cock," he cackled, "with a twinkle in her eye!"

A young soldier ran up to the sleigh and spoke to the fool.

"Take your master's camera. He dropped it in the snow by the station."

"Keep it, keep it, my friend," Herr Grunewald urged the soldier. "Take some snaps for your girl." And then he sang, "So she'll jump on your cock with a twinkle in her eye!"

The soldier shouted his thanks over the train whistles that required him to return to the platform.

"More horses for our boys, Polack shitface," Herr Grunewald said before he fell into a deep sleep. "*Juden* ponies! *Juden* proof!"

✦ ✦ ✦

As soon as the exhausted horse crossed over the former snow-map of Poland, Frau Grunewald and two of her maids rushed out the door.

"Witold! What's happened to you?"

The smell of alcohol, garlic, and sickness overwhelmed the Frau as she shone her lamp on her husband's placid face. Bits of sausage rind were frozen fast to his chin.

"Help me, please," Frau Grunewald said to the girls. "Shake him."

The two girls rubbed Herr Grunewald's head with their warm hands, and he began singing again. "And she jumped on his cock with a twinkle in her eye." He sang first in Polish, then in German. "Her little teeny eyes . . ."

Frau Grunewald dropped her lamp. Before the wick started to sizzle, she threw several stones from Poland's onetime borders at her husband's coat — and when these missiles failed to gain his attention, she dropped a log (a former Panzer division, you'll recall) onto his stomach. With Tadek's help, the girls finally managed to get the master's legs out of the sleigh, but they all moved away when Frau Grunewald picked up another log that, when it fell on Witold's back, sounded like a mallet hitting flesh.

"Holy Mother of God," he stammered after this last blow. "Enough! It's me." The Polish maids took a bruised and remorseful Herr Grunewald up the steps. Once out of his wife's throwing range, he took the opportunity to squeeze the buttocks of the younger one. "Do you like the song, little one? Makes a pretty tune, yes?"

Frau Grunewald sank into the snow close to the sleigh. She had neither the strength nor the will to throw another stone at her husband's back, but she did smash the lamp with a small log. It was this cracking sound that made Witold Grunewald postpone the trip his hand was making over the maid's dress. He staggered back down the steps and hoisted his wife to her feet.

"Come in, my love — the cold is bad for you. We'll have a drop of brandy and apologize all night." (Of course, Witold also wanted to tell her about the two thousand per day in Modlin.)

"Witold," she said in Polish. "To think about what's happened!"

"What? My short trip to see our soldiers?"

Frau Grunewald choked and cried. When these terrible sounds subsided, she told him that the wireless reported that the battle for Stalingrad was over. Herr Grunewald's first impulse, even in the howling wind, was to spin his wife like a top and shout out praises to God. But the Frau soon corrected him by reporting the details she'd heard over the evening broadcast from Berlin. And that's when Herr Grunewald vomited up sausage, soup, and the bile that came from mixing cherry brandy and vodka.

"All of them?" he cried, falling into the snow. "We've lost all of them to those animals?"

Frau Grunewald nodded, then knelt next to her husband's head. "Tadek," the Frau commanded. "Help us!"

It took Tadeusz and both of the maids at least twenty minutes to get the master and mistress upstairs. "It's better for you not to understand," Herr Grunewald said to his fool in a calm voice. "Better, better, better!"

✦ ✦ ✦

Early the next morning, hours before Herr Grunewald was well enough to leave his chamber pot, Chaim Turkow faced the eastern wall of his freezing hut and quietly said the benedictions. If the words of the prayers were difficult to remember, the sentences he later wrote in Yiddish on a piece of scrap paper came easily enough. "My Dear Parents and Sisters," he began in a letter he must have known would never go anywhere. "I, Chaim Turkow, am alive." When he at last finished writing — he mentioned the pigs, the odd cries of the horses being loaded into cattlecars in Modlin, the arms he saw between two leather valises, the babushka, the loneliness and silence he felt were killing him — he hid the letter behind a loose slat in the back of the Black Madonna's gilt-edged frame.

Three days later, a despondent and unshaven Witold Grunewald announced that, "given the tactical reverses in the east," he was going to Warsaw to sell some of the family's things. In an argument heard throughout the house, Frau Grunewald said she would rather die in the snow than be forced to part with her mother's cherished paintings and her family's valuable Persian rugs, which she, not Witold or his idiot ancestors, had brought to the drafty estate house in Poland.

Herr Grunewald banged his fist on the table. "Without cash to leave for Sweden, we hang," he shouted. "It's all over!" He also said he was taking the fool with him to help carry and watch over the heavier goods. Fräulein Grunewald ran upstairs and tried to hide her jewelry and the platinum jewelry box given to her by the late lieutenant.

Elzbieta and Tadeusz packed the precious Grunewald cargo into the sleigh while their master tried to console his wife and daughter. Worried about his safekeeping on the ride to Modlin and the further rail trip to Warsaw, the cook made her Tadek pray with her over the rosary beads she wrapped around his hands. "Believe in Him," she kept saying. "Every day, believe and remember His sacrifice."

When the old woman finally fell asleep in her chair, Chaim Turkow used his last hour on the Grunewald estate to sew a pocket inside his coat lining large enough to hold three pencils he took from Herr Grunewald's desk, the two photographs from Nowy Dwor, and all of the unfinished sketches of his family.

9

I T'S QUITE SIMPLE : everything can be arranged once you have a plan as well thought out as Witold Grunewald's — for if he ever had any fears about the prospect of his imminent execution after the surrender of so many divisions in Russia, they were soon forgotten when he began to make a fortune in Warsaw. The long train ride to the capital with his fool convinced him that he'd been much too hasty in seeing the end of the war merely because of "tactical reverses." To be sure, he made a point of chatting with the German officers who filled the first-class compartment on the Warsaw express, using all of his charm (and cigars) to discover the truth.

"Things are going well?" he would casually ask after sharing a drink from his flask with several officers returning from the front.

The officers chuckled amongst themselves, puffed long and hard at their expensive cigars. "Ah, but do you see us running back to Berlin, my friend?" one of the officers said. "Aren't we here with you, doing our job? Don't we seem content? Do you see any Soviet tankmen chasing our train?"

Can you imagine the feeling of relief that rushed through Witold Grunewald's mind? Although the officers looked at one another — once again, they had to play-act in front of an ignorant *Volksdeutscher* from the provinces — he heard what he desperately needed to hear: All was well, more or less, at the front. His wife and daughter would not be raped and killed by rampaging partisans or Bolshie-Yid swine, and the security of his beautiful estate was guaranteed by the words of noble officers and gentlemen. "I was once considered for a sub-ministerial post," he bragged to every German in his compartment. "It's only a matter of time until Hans Frank himself sends me an invitation to come to the Wawel Castle!"

While the train drew closer to Warsaw, past villages and roads clogged with army trucks, tanks, and cattlecars, Witold Grunewald turned his attention to making money.

"Warsaw is there for the picking," one of the officers said. "There is gold coming in from all over Europe."

"And it all came interest-free from the Yids," another said. "Beautiful stuff!"

This same officer, soon drunk on Herr Grunewald's brandy, spoke about the amazing opportunities available to men of "commercial instinct." And when the officer listened to Herr Grunewald's listing of the goods he had brought with him (though Witold never mentioned his ultimate plan in fleeing his estate), he slapped his new friend on the back.

"It will be magic," the officer said. "Your Persian rugs will sell for three times their original value, and your wife's cheap necklaces will change into coins before your eyes! Wealth will float down from the heavens when you stack those tiny oil paintings in some merchant's shop. If it's cash you want, you'll soon drown in it."

Herr Grunewald thanked the officer for his advice and promised, "on our mutual Reich honor," to pay him a visit in Warsaw so that they might put some of this cash to good use

with a few Polish whores. "I know just where to go, too," Herr
Grunewald said. "A club where the cleanest thighs in Warsaw
stretch before one." Then he sang, "And she'll jump on your
cock with a . . ."

Witold Grunewald took his leave from his fellow passengers
to check on Tadeusz, who was riding in the baggage car with
the trunks and boxes, and as he excitedly told the fool what the
officers had just said, he devised his ingenious scheme. It was
simple in design, easy to carry out — such a work of art that
Herr Grunewald promised himself he would never again doubt
the eventual victory of the Reich. I will become a Pole by
name, he thought, and then I'll store my tradegoods in (he
was proudest of this one) some convent or church. God willing,
I'll find the Jews' gold the good officer said was available to
all but the witless.

✦   ✦   ✦

So that is how Pan Grunowski and his mute servant came to be
housed at the convent run by the Sisters of Saint Angelica —
far enough away (five kilometers) from the center to be safe
from thieves and the walled-off area where the world had the
good sense to stockpile what was left of Warsaw's Jews.

Everything worked out according to plan. Pan Grunowski
hired a driver and truck at the station, ordered to be driven to
the first church the Pole could find, and asked the elderly
priest how to find a suitable place "where a believing son of
the Holy Virgin" might find a quiet convent to use as a "place
of spiritual retreat in these troubled times." The priest looked
at the silent youth accompanying the generous petitioner in
search of solace, then carefully counted the offered coins. He
wrote down the names of two convents in the far suburbs.

"Maybe your servant will find a voice from Christ's message," the priest whispered to Pan Grunowski. "True, true, Father," came the reply. "Another reason why we've come so far from home."

From the back of the truck, Chaim caught his first sight of the capital between the canvas flaps of the ramshackle vehicle. With every bump, the flaps opened to reveal burned-out buildings, twisted tramrails, boulevards filled with Poles selling everything imaginable, huge mounds of crushed cinderblocks. Poles seemed to carry on their affairs without noticing the destruction or the soldiers on every corner. "Terrible, terrible," he heard Grunewald mumbling to the driver in the cab. "How did it ever come to this?"

The truck wove back and forth through narrow streets. Sadly, the first convent Pan Grunowski came to was no longer occupied; the former convent house teetered over the edge of a crater designed by someone's powerful bomb. Disappointing, of course, but Pan Grunowski took heart when the driver told him that the second convent — a few kilometers farther out from the center, in the Praga district — was "cleaner."

"But is it in one piece, idiot?" he asked. "Or are you taking me to another ditch?"

The Pole laughed and readjusted his fare to compensate for the longer ride to the quiet street, where, partially hidden by some large oak trees, the Gothic convent stood unharmed by bombs or fire. "This is it," Witold yelled to the driver when the truck pulled next to the gray stone walls and a large iron gate. "I'll pay any price to stay here. Unload the goods, Tadek. They can't deny me here."

The Sisters didn't refuse, agreeing to the wealthy and spiritually starved gentleman's request, especially pleased by the offer of his servant as groundskeeper and the gift of a few trinkets Pan Grunowski quickly found in one of the crates.

"Whatever you wish to make of him, Mother," Witold Grunowski added, pushing the fool in front of her. "He never complains. I, of course, will be attending to my religious duties by giving all of my worldly wealth to various churches in the city, not to mention the long hours I plan for my prayers. My absence during daylight hours will be the fulfillment of a cherished dream: to pray and give charity."

The stone outbuilding the Mother Superior offered was perfect, too. Set back from the main convent building between a garden and a toolshed, its two rooms had once been used to quarter visiting priests who used to come to celebrate mass for the Sisters. Pan Grunowski was happy to learn that the building's cellar would be a secure place for his crates and the fool.

When the Mother Superior took note of the loaded truck by her front gate, she turned red with expectation. "So many offerings, Pan Grunowski. Surely, you are a saintly man to give so much to those in need."

"I do what I can, Sister. Only what I can."

When they came into the courtyard, Pan Grunowski dropped to his knees and genuflected in front of a small statue of the Virgin. His eyes swollen with religious passion, Pan Grunowski finally rose and gave the nun a small silver cross. "A priceless piece, Sister. Please, accept it with my thanks."

Their contract agreed upon, the two good Catholics retreated to the Mother Superior's study. "Bring your servant with you," she said. "All I have is some poor tea."

It took Pan Grunowski all of ten minutes within the threadbare, damp room to see what had to be done to firm up the security he needed in his religious quest. First, he would part with a scratched crystal goblet, and then, with an additional gift of a worthless Persian rug, he would always have the honorable lady in his debt. "Close your eyes, Sister Marysia. I am about to attack the chill in your room."

Pan Grunowski whispered instructions to Tadeusz. The Pole left the Sister's room and returned with a rug that once kept Fräulein Grunewald's feet warm.

"Unroll it when I count to three," Pan Grunowski ordered. "She'll love it."

And so she did.

During the course of their friendly chat, the nun learned everything about the fool who followed each instruction without question or expression. Pan Grunowski explained how the youth came to be with him ("A foundling given to me by our parish priest. I've raised the boy like a son"), the nature of his mental infirmities, his eternal silence (humming was not mentioned), his way with the pigs and other livestock, the day he took such decent photographs.

"Just one thing, Sister Marysia. He has a habit of wandering off. I worry so about him that I would be grateful if you kept him within these holy walls while I am a pilgrim in this sad city. Lord knows what my wife and I would do if any harm came to him. Believe me, he's a little puppy, really — bursting over with love at the simplest kindness!"

Sister Marysia was so moved by Witold Grunowski's words, she pledged her vigilance for as long as necessary. "He will never leave the grounds, good sir. My Sisters, and Lord Jesus, will protect him."

Pan Grunowski left the convent each morning with the items he selected for the day's sale: a few oil paintings, several rugs, perhaps some of the smaller chairs or some lusterless pearls. Over the many months he spent with the Sisters, Pan Grunowski quickly accumulated gold and silver. The more he made, the less he thought about the war. He never sold too much on any given day and never bored his German customers (almost all of them were officers) with incessant chitchat about politics or the crumbling eastern front.

This lucrative business took a good deal of time and travel back and forth between Warsaw and the Grunewald estate. And no matter how worthless or inconsequential the goods Pan Grunowski brought to the capital, there was always some official with a doctorate who wished to take something, anything, back home with him to the Fatherland. Antique mirrors went for twenty times their original price; colorless tapestries the Grunewald maids never cleaned were prized as "superb examples of Polish artisanship"; even the stereoscopic slides of "Winter Scenes from Zakopane" brought a good price from a Luftwaffe captain with one eye. This war, the *Volksdeutscher* knew, was giving him all he would need to buy the best apartment to be had in Stockholm.

✦   ✦   ✦

Alone in the cellar with Grunowski's crates and canvas-draped paintings, Chaim Turkow couldn't remember from one day to the next if he'd prayed. He'd forgotten the dates of the holidays. If he tried to sketch on the few sheets of paper he had left, his fingers stumbled over lines; the half-drawn faces were unrecognizable. He slept without dreaming. Sometimes he wet the cot.

One night, after Pan Grunowski had kept him up past midnight shining and polishing a set of silver-plated forks, Chaim began to tear at his own scalp, pulling out clumps of dull blond hair until his head was covered with bloody patches. Seeing this madness, Grunowski held his servant's head under the faucet and slapped the idiot's back with a walking stick.

During the following week, while Pan Grunowski left for his estate to fetch another wagonload of family treasures, Chaim began to sleep without bedclothes or covers. He thought he was losing his mind. He lay against the wall and scratched his hands on the rough stones. The chill made his back stiffen and his arms feel like they were being pulled from their sockets. He tried — and failed — to add simple sums; he had no idea which season followed the long winter; only three of the nine Jewish elders' names were more than a dull memory. Think of a word you know, he told himself. Or your age. Try and move your right foot: feel something!

Soon he was overtaken by convulsions and nausea, accompanied by a pain that seemed to be moving away from his head toward his legs. He thought that if he could raise himself against the wall the cold brick would help lower his fever, but breathing was becoming difficult and he was afraid to move. He sat for hours on the floor, trying to make out the shapes of Pan Grunowski's many crates, the steel cot, a broken washbasin. He closed his eyes and awoke only to take his meals in the dining hall, where, as always, he sat alone in the corner under a large wooden crucifix.

Somehow, despite the aching in his legs, on the third day Chaim Turkow found his boots and a thick rope to tie around his trousers. His head began to clear after he pulled himself up. Nothing was as important as going outside. It didn't matter to him that he'd forgotten his fool's name or his coat.

The convent's courtyard was empty and covered by a late

spring snow. Chaim saw the haze by the gas lamp and followed the stone path to the bench where — as fool or Jew? — he usually sat after meals. Although the cold froze his sweat, he paid no heed to his body. With a trembling hand he traced a design in the snow. The stick moved easily back and forth. The singing, of course, was helpful — a long "la, mee, nah" made for a fine circle and some and oblong shapes, and a "boo, za, za, boom" resulted in some lines. And when the sky over the convent's eastern wall let a few purple rays illuminate some details, Chaim, now on his knees, drew a large-brimmed hat on top of Moishe Turkow's head.

Aided by the increasing light, Chaim finished shaping the expansive figure with his hands, and crumbled a bit of coal-dust over the innkeeper's jacket and hat. Chaim stretched out next to the snow figure: he might have been dreaming or letting his mind slip away, just as he'd let his voice die (humming excepted) because he, Chaim Turkow, was once entrusted with some photographs and sketches. So, there he lay in the snow: dirty from the coal dust, the dangerous morning light around him, his hands touching the midsection of a very good swimmer and father. He turned on his side and grabbed for the snow-hand of Moishe Turkow. "Take the handkerchief, Papa," he said. "We should wave at the women who are watching us!"

Chaim felt the ground give way to their leaps and jumps. They, father and son, wearing their best clothes and the good shoes from Warsaw, moved faster and faster. Together their pace was much quicker than the poor musician's ability to keep up.

"Don't let go," Chaim sang. "Manya is cheering for us. Ram, ba, ba, bamba . . . lowda, deeda, dum."

Chaim looked up when his father's hand pulled away. He kept singing, certain his sisters were laughing at him. He ignored the woman who'd embarrassed the rabbi by crossing over to be with the men. "It's not permitted," the Jews were saying to this brazen woman. "How can she do such a thing?"

"Stay with the bride," he told her. "The women must keep her company."

A dark babushka brushed close to his face. "Shh," came the whisper. "Shh."

His eyelids were wiped with the warm cloth, and Chaim Turkow took in enough light to see that the dark-haired servant girl who served him his meals from the Sisters' kitchen was also at the wedding. She helped him stand in the shallow ditch he dug for himself during his dance with the innkeeper and the dozen other men who, though they were now running away, had sung and danced as well as Moishe Turkow. "Where is my father?" he asked. "We shouldn't waste good music."

The girl threw a blanket over him. She jabbed him repeatedly with her finger because he wouldn't stop babbling in Yiddish. "Don't say anything more," the girl said. "They'll hear!"

Whoosh. The girl, this wedding girl who didn't know any better than to cross over to the men's side — this girl was pulling him away from everyone. Chaim knew his family would think him mad for letting a girl push him this way and that. *Whoosh*, she moved again. But Milutsky wouldn't care at all. No. How many times had the printer told him how he'd danced with different women? Freethinkers without wigs, the kind who'd rub your back in public and smoke in the market square! Once with Rosa Luxemburg, he said, when she was beautiful, he said, for the beautiful Red star was a bit drunk after working so hard.

"Shh!"

The melting snow seeped through the fool's clothing. He was helped down the steps into the dark passage that led to his room. The musicians stopped playing as the girl gave him one last push toward the cot.

"Shh. It's all right now."

While she washed his face, blackened by coal dust, she told him not to worry anymore. Chaim mumbled some names, and then the girl said her name was Anya and that once his fever passed she would tell him how to find a place where there were still some Jews left. Chaim began to call for Milutsky.

The girl put the cloth over his eyes. "Shh," she whispered again, cradling his head. "I know the way to the wall."

And everything she said was in Yiddish.

10

SISTER MARYSIA ordered the dark-haired girl to stay with the servant of their wealthy patron, pray over him if he vomited into the bedpan, and, of course, to wrap the poor boy's fingers with the rosary beads. "Call the priest only if he gags and turns blue," she reminded the girl, "and always wash your hands after you leave." She also advised the girl to close her eyes and hold a chamber pot between his legs every few hours.

Since the girl had permission to tend the fool wherever she thought best, she came to him every night, listened to his garbled, crazy stories about a steam bath and a sister — her name was Manya? — who drew pictures of tigers. Yet whenever this Jew was about to finish a sentence, his fever or his madness took over and he fell into a deep, mumbling sleep. Later, when his fever subsided, it was Anya who asked him to repeat everything: the name of his town, his family's name, the way in which a printer let a blond Jew practice painting and drawing. Once, maybe twice, she felt that her own cold body might help bring down his temperature, so she lay over him and put her head on his chest. "Tell me again," she said. "Tell me about those people you knew by the river."

The night before Witold Grunewald returned from his

estate to the Sisters of Saint Angelica and his Polack fool, Chaim Turkow's fever finally broke. The ache in his head became a dull throb and his eyes were no longer covered by a sticky film. For the first time in days, he remembered the words of the morning benediction as well as how to add six and seven.

Chaim was alone in the cellar when he came up with the correct sum of thirteen. He had no recollection of being in the snow with Moishe Turkow, nor did he remember his dance or an old man yelling at some woman for being brazen and without shame. With his throat cleared of phlegm and his scalp itching a bit as it healed, Chaim sat up in the cot and waited. The week that had just passed meant nothing to him since, as you've probably guessed, he thought he'd been sleeping for only one night and awakened with a bad headache and a stiff back, a few awful nightmares, and sore knuckles from beads someone had wrapped around his left hand.

The girl came into the cellar so suddenly, Tadeusz Kazanowski made an awkward bow while trying to cover himself.

"No, you don't have to do that anymore," she said in Polish. "We have only a few minutes left."

Tadeusz pointed to his mouth, grunted, and shook his head — a fool's sign in front of a Polish girl. He crossed himself and jiggled the rosary. If the girl hadn't come close to his cot, he would have acted the fool and thrown himself to the floor and begged at her feet.

She pulled the beads away from Tadeusz. "Chaim Turkow, son of Moishe — I took you out of the snow. I saw your dance."

Stunned at now hearing Yiddish, not knowing anything about a dance or how this Pole knew about Moishe Turkow,

Chaim pretended to gag. He ripped at his hair. Was it over? Had Moishe Turkow had finally come?

"Stop it," she said. "I know everything. Stop it and listen to me."

The girl ran to the door. When she didn't hear anyone coming, she told him about his fever and the names. She gave him a tiny scroll of paper, wound as tightly as a thin cigarette.

"I copied everything you said. You sang some nonsense rhymes . . . it's here, you see. And your names, many names."

Chaim unwound the scroll and read the minuscule Yiddish script covering every section of the paper. Names. The "Shu, sha" minus a letter or two to save space. "Why did you do this?" he asked, overwhelmed at seeing and hearing Yiddish. "Why?"

"Spare me the need to pity you," she said. "So you've lost a few names and a voice. I play the poor Polish girl without parents. Three weeks I hid under the steps of this convent until they took me in to serve meals and clean their outhouse. I even let myself be touched by your Grunowski while the nuns slept. I eat bread, have some air. What difference does it make how we live? Air is air. Get dressed and trust me. Your master is taking you away today."

Pan Grunowski's laughter echoed in the stone hallway outside the cellar door. The girl put her hand over the fool's mouth and pushed him toward the cot. She emptied a bucket of dirty water and began scrubbing the stones with a rag. The laughter, and the softer voice of Sister Marysia, faded.

"You're returning to the country," the girl said. "I heard him arrange a time with his driver. He told the old man he'd had enough of the nuns. They were laughing and drinking."

The girl wiped her filthy hands over her apron. She slid on the wet floor toward the door and listened. Her breasts still ached from her last time with the Pole who ruled this Jew's life; but this one from Nowy Dwor wouldn't understand any of this, she thought. All he had were names, stories about pictures! She didn't have her wedding band any longer or the green beads her husband gave her when their daughter was born.

"And when you were bad off three nights again, I stayed with you for a long time. That's when you said 'they' were torn by an animal."

"Sketches, a packet of photographs?"

"How should I know?"

The laughter returned. Chaim and the girl could see Grunowski's boots framed by the narrow window grate below the ceiling. "Come closer," she said.

She held out her arm and pulled this fool toward her. "Look, whatever you are from Nowy Dwor, I haven't any more paper. You look at my arm while I do this."

She scratched lines along her forearm with a fingernail until the skin became scored with deep red marks. Chaim tried to stop her, but she smacked his face with the wet rag; then, making even more lines, she pinched herself to raise welts in several spots. She never cried out when the longest and deepest scratch began to bleed.

"You're in Warsaw, yes? You understand this?"

"I know where I am," Chaim said.

"Maybe you do. And do you know how close you are to what's left of the ghetto?"

The word meant nothing to Chaim. Once again, the girl wiped her arm with the greasy rag after making a last X with her fingernail. "Here is where the convent is" — her finger moved to another scratch, across what was a brilliantly red Vistula — "and the Jews are here. You can even take a tram."

As her finger moved from wrist to elbow, she showed the Jew where Poles sometimes smuggled food to those inside the walled area. When she impressed a smaller *x* that cut across a vein, she said, "At this place, they say, people left the ghetto and boarded the trains. New tracks came in '41. This is the old cemetery for the Jews."

The blood from the girl's arm trickled over her apron and ran down her legs. "Here, here, you see — some of them are in here!"

"How many are in this place?" he asked, reaching for her arm. "Where are they from?" The girl ran to the door, listened to the laughing voices — Pan Grunowski was in the middle of a long, humorous anecdote — and again fell to the floor. Maybe a minute or two left to tell this foolish, lucky Jew what all of Poland knew or suspected.

"I don't know. The Sisters talk when I clean and they say how awful it is. They say the Germans won't let anyone get too close to the walls. Last month I carried a sack of flour from a shop close to the edge of the ghetto, and the shopowner told the Sister who was with me what a good job was being done by the Germans. Then he points to the wall and smiles. 'Excuse me, Sister,' he says. 'The Germans are shits, but sometimes even shit can be useful!' "

"Who are you? Why do you tell me this?"

The girl sloshed some water on the stone floor and hid her face behind the iron frame. "Because my name is Anya Kravitz and you've been a fool too long."

Pan Grunowski's voice was growing louder.

"So the man with the dog takes the woman outside — " Pan Grunowski was now yelling between bursts of laughter to the Sister and the Polish driver. They were very close now.

Anya rinsed the map of her skin in the bucket. "Your master said he had to make a delivery somewhere close to here, not far from the ghetto. So you know how to draw, Chaim Turkow! You know about sketching. Slip away and go see."

Even a wise man from a small town, let alone a Jew playing an idiot, would have asked the same question as Chaim Turkow. "Do you know any of my people? Have their names been mentioned?"

The sweet smell of toilet water reached them a second before the heavy-booted foot kicked open the door. Anya Kravitz swirled the dirty water everywhere and whispered, "Lose your mind again. Shh."

Pan Grunowski nearly lost his footing on the slippery stone floor. "Better now?" he bellowed at Tadeusz.

The fool nodded and stood up. Yes, better.

"Then this girl will see to it that you have some soup in the kitchen. Eat and come back here to pack the crates. We leave in two hours. By the way, wash yourself and splash some of this over you."

Pan Grunowski tossed a small bottle of toilet water on the cot. "You smell like that damn pail in the corner. And be sure to douse my crates with whatever's left. These are gifts for important people."

Sister Marysia walked into the cellar and immediately covered her mouth with a lace handkerchief. Anya, seeing the Mother Superior so uncomfortable, started to fan the nun with a dry rag. The girl meant well — her safety depended upon small acts of consideration — but she was not prepared for the Sister's reaction.

"Look at her, Pan Grunowski. You see how she parades her filth in front of us!"

Ever the cooperative Christian pilgrim, Witold Grunowski tried to stop Sister Marysia from striking the girl, who, it seemed, had bright splotches of fresh blood running down her leg. The girl's apron was wet and spotted red.

"Sister, Sister, please. She's just had a little accident. You know as well as I how they live in the countryside! Young Tadek, for instance, still doesn't know when he has to — if you'll excuse the expression — take care of his own business. Let her wash and put on a little of my cologne. Simpletons must be pitied, not punished."

"But no regard for common cleanliness, Pan Grunowski — and in here, in front of a boy!"

Sister Marysia wailed for help and tried to escape Pan Grunowski's grip; the girl fell to her knees and began to cry. She buried her face in the dirty rag and dipped her apron into the bucket. Chaim thought he saw her rub something on one of the stones. Several nuns heard the shouting and had congregated at the door. Sister Marysia snapped her fingers and told the nuns to bathe the girl in a cold tub and get rid of the stains.

Pan Grunowski took it upon himself to end this scene by offering one more donation to the nuns' comfort and security. "And don't trouble yourself about my feelings, dear Sister," he pleaded, "as there's no reason for me to think less of this refuge because of one unclean servant."

Somehow, the strength of his argument acted as a balm to

Sister Marysia. She smoothed her rumpled habit and pulled the silver crucifix around her neck. Her lace handkerchief fluttered around her nose like a white bird.

"This is for you and the others to remember me in your prayers," Pan Grunowski said to the Sister. "Now, perhaps we could share some tea before my journey home?"

On his way to the Sister's room, Pan Grunowski met his driver in the courtyard.

"Watch the idiot pack, and watch that skinny girl the others are washing in the courtyard," he told the driver. "Twelve crates are here; twelve must go out with us. Your supper money, friend, depends on a good eye."

Tadeusz began to tie the ropes over the crates, but his fingers were clumsy and the knots were too loose. The driver made him do each knot over again before he let him take a rest on the cot.

"Now put that whore smell on you like he said to do."

The rest of the time in the cellar was spent waiting — surrounded by the overpowering odor of violets mixed with latrine disinfectant — for Pan Grunowski. The Polish driver smoked and said he didn't give a fuck about anything.

"Up, up, you two," Pan Grunowski shouted when he returned a little later. "I told you to get these things on the truck." Despite his abruptness, Witold Grunowski was actually in a very good mood. He joked with the driver, threw a kiss to the horrified novice who stood watching the men from the gate. He told Tadeusz to dress warmly. "If we do our work well, Tadek, we can be home in two days."

The driver tripped over the bucket. "Wipe this up, you," he yelled at Tadeusz, "before I kill myself here."

Tadeusz dropped to the floor. He wiped a dry and clear path

for the driver, but stopped just before a wet ring left by the girl's bucket. Scrawled in the dirt tracked into the cellar by Sister Marysia and Pan Grunowski, he saw the Yiddish words "Anya-Vilna."

11

YOU SAY THIS STORY is incredible, don't you? You say:
Here is a story about a Polish Jew (*we've* forgotten his
age by now) whose father was wise enough to send
him away from a small town where the future played itself
out one afternoon in the market square. And what happens?
The boy obeys his father without question, takes along some
photographs and sketches of dancing children and frightened
old men, hides for years in a place where he doesn't suffer,
becomes a fool with a pleasing hum, and eventually goes to
Warsaw and meets a Jewish girl from Vilna (where there
used to be many, many Jews and a good deal of studying)
who tells him: Look at my arm, I'm going to scratch a map
on my skin that will show you where the Jews are being
hidden. Behind a wall, she says. In a ghetto.

You pause and find someone you trust. "This is too much
to believe," you say. "This Chaim Turkow — if such a person
ever existed — doesn't know what has been happening in his
own country. Impossible!" Then you turn on us. It's obvious
we've insulted your knowledge of recent history — indeed,
we dare to condescend to someone who has seen the photographs, the newsreels, those children's drawings of butterflies
in Terezin, read at least a few books, and maybe, as a sidelight

to a holiday tour of Europe, walked solemnly through a memorial museum filled with the shoes and suitcases of a vanished people.

Still, *try* to believe us when we ask you to be patient as we tell you how, in the middle of Poland's premier city, on a day when the sky was clear and blue, Chaim Turkow was less than a half-kilometer away from the second welt on Anya of Vilna's arm.

✦ ✦ ✦

Witold Grunowski occasionally looked through the small window of his driver's truck to check on the fool who sat next to four packing crates promised to a buyer somewhere in Warsaw. "Hold on, Tadek," he shouted when the truck veered around a few corners. "We're nearly there."

Sitting alongside Roman, his Polish driver, in the cab, Witold Grunowski was in a splendid mood. He never yelled when the Pole took a wrong turning (most traffic signs were in German, or, worse, defaced). With only a few expensive odds and ends to unload before he returned to his estate with his ten pouches of assorted currencies and gold pieces, Pan Grunowski felt good enough to sing a few of his bawdier Polish songs when the driver stopped to buy some food from a cart or some vodka from a bootlegger. Why bother with details, Witold told himself, when my business is finally done with? So what if the Polack stops for a ring of sausage or a half-liter of vodka? The more he drinks, the more he'll forget his wages — besides, the fool in the back has to have something!

"Eat," Pan Grunowski said, passing back a large slice of the smelly sausage through the rear window of the cab.

"Today is a victory for us, Tadek. Soon we'll both get to sleep where we belong."

When the driver pulled the truck off the street and parked, Pan Grunowski, his bladder and bowels aching from the vodka (not to mention the purple rash around his crotch he'd noticed the day before), bolted from the truck and ran to a small square where people sat and watched their children. "Piss for your life, sir," the driver yelled outside the grove of oaks where Pan Grunowski moaned inside the public lavatory. "This is the last time we stop."

Chaim had no idea where he was. The streets were crowded with soldiers and peddlers; a group of children chased a ball and kicked clumps of melting snow; young girls walked hand-in-hand. Even in the buildings with gaping holes, Poles still found a few dry places to sit and take in a bit of sun, though everyone avoided the beggars who grabbed at them from dark corners. The driver returned from taunting Pan Grunowski — Witold had yet to emerge from the wooden privy in the square — and sat next to the fool.

"Despite everything, the pretty ladies still come out. Grunt your answer and I promise not to tell your employer, boy: Have you ever fucked a lady?" Tadeusz stared blankly. "You can be a man with me, you know," Roman continued, snapping his fingers in front of the fool's eyes. "Not even a few sheep or goats back on that big estate where you come from?"

What could Tadeusz do but grunt and take a sip of the driver's cloudy vodka?

"Good and soft for you, blue eyes? Here, have some more."

An iron fence surrounded the square. A few couples sat on the rotting wooden benches and held hands. A newspaper vendor sold Polish and German papers, and the only disturbance in this unusually placid scene came from the locked privy where Pan Grunowski felt the effects of too much raw sausage and pepper-vodka. "Can't you see I'm in a bad way," he yelled at anyone who rattled the privy's door. "Have mercy on a sick brother."

A snowball whizzed by the truck, and Roman, ducking too late, caught the full force of the missile on his chest. "Son of a bitch!" But he was too drunk now to run after the child who hid behind the fence. "Gypsy bastard," he screamed, wiping the dirty snow from his collar and neck. He threw an empty bottle toward the fence. "Fuck off, little one. Enjoy your fun while you're still on this side of the wall."

Tadeusz began pulling at his nose, just as he'd seen Elzbieta do whenever she talked about the Jews. He stood in front of Roman, giving the Jew-sign and looking puzzled. The driver ducked a few more snowballs. He was about to chase the children when he noticed the fool's antics.

"For Christ's sake, what?" (More nosepulling.) "You don't know, do you? No one's given you the pleasure of knowing, right?"

Tadeusz held up his arms and pulled at his nose until it hurt. He even did a poor imitation of a Yid's dance. The driver laughed.

"Why not, yes? Even a sheep-screwer like you should have the chance to get a little view, maybe a whiff to boot. I know just the place."

The driver's huge chest heaved and rolled with a series of garlic-laced belches. He pointed to the privy.

"So what if the old man finishes before we're through. He'll wait if he wants me to haul his stuff. Come on, then, eh? It's not far. You'll see something you can take back to the country and I'll get a few trinkets. Come on, I'll show you what I mean."

The driver closed the truck's flaps and locked the doors.

"Stay close to me, boy. It won't take but a few minutes to get you to stop poking your nose."

+ + +

The driver led Chaim through the square, where street merchants were doing a brisk business in scraps of cloth, onions, stale bread. An old woman sat crossed-legged on a low cart, begging for coins or food. She spat at anyone who ignored her wailing, and tugged at Roman's trousers when he walked past. "Ease my soul and Christ will love ye," she cried.

"Take this, sister," he said as he dropped the empty bottle into her lap. "It's worth a copper to someone." The woman spat into the bottle and threw it back at the driver's boots.

The driver and the fool passed a cinema hall, more beggars, a score of destroyed buildings and courtyards. The Pole carefully navigated through streets that became narrower and dirtier, with sewage leaking from broken pipes and dripping from clogged gutters. Cats fought over half-eaten pigeons dragged from the pools of black water. Roman waved to some young women who were taking advantage of the sunlight to hang their gray laundry.

The driver stopped twenty meters away from a high red brick wall by a three-story building. He tugged on the fool's coat, and then he pulled long and hard on his own bulbous, red nose.

"Here we are, friend. You can't get any closer than this to those filthy bastards on the other side — you can't, that is, if you aren't me and don't know how to do it! I live in this place. And so long as you want to see Yids hoppin' about, you might as well have a real treat and watch 'em like I do."

This said, the driver took the measure of the fool's skinny

body, turning him around like someone inspecting a hanging sausage. "You'll fit," he said. "No doubt about it, you'll slide through easier than a stallion's prick in a spring mare!"

To save time, he led Chaim under a wire fence in front of the building. While the driver fumbled with some keys in an old lock, Chaim read the Polish names penciled in over the former residents' calling cards: Ziarek over Bloom. Przemecka obscuring a Dr. Orenshtayn. Rabowska, A., not even bothering to block out the raised gold letters of Pinkus Rosen, Adventurer.

"This is a fine place to live," the driver said when they finally entered the musty hallway and descended the stairs. "Everything recently vacated, if you know what I mean." The smells of boiled turnips and dampness soured the building. Chaim, an inch away from the driver's back, stepped in a pool of cat urine that ran down several steps.

Following the driver, Chaim stumbled over broken wooden boxes, strands of rusty wire, vegetables starting to rot in open bins, rags stacked against the brick walls. A stub of a lit candle revealed the driver's treasures as he carefully checked each box and bin, selecting a dozen or so vegetables and stale breads, then stuffing them into a canvas sack. Next, like a good tailor measuring an ignorant customer, he sized up the fool from several angles.

"Suck in your stomach," he said, before punching him hard. The boy (or so the driver thought him to be) doubled over into just the right size. "Turn around and take this sack. I'm going to show you how to see all those noses, little man. But since nothin' comes free, you'll have to do a little trading for me at the end of a special sewer I know that goes right under the wall."

The Pole took Chaim back up the stairway and out a rear door into a small courtyard that was very close to the high wall Chaim saw when they first came to the building. "That's where we go, nose-lover," the driver said, pointing to an old wooden shed between several refuse cans. "That's where you get to see 'em dance."

Still carrying the sack of food, Tadeusz followed the Pole into the deserted shed. "Here's what you do, friend," he said to the fool once they were safely inside. "I'm going to move some bricks over there by that pile of junk. You'll see a big hole, like a pisspot in the best hotels, only much bigger. You climb down the rope ladder I got attached to the top of the hole. About twenty meters off, when you get to the bottom of the pipe, you'll find another ladder. When you get there, you pull yourself up, knock a couple a times at the sewer hatch until one of the Yids moves it for you. Since you can't say nothin', let him pull up the sack of food and drop down the money. Take a look when the Jew lifts the sewer cover, but hurry up because I got to brush you off and get back to the one who can't keep his pants up."

The driver knew his business, too: the bricks were moved and there was a large hole. With the sack over his shoulder, Tadeusz held on to the rope and went down. No need for a light, he was told. There'll be plenty of light after the nose moves the hatch.

"There's always some Yid hanging around at the other end waiting for someone to show up with the stuff. Don't worry, the only real problem you got is if all the Krauts in Warsaw shit at once!"

The driver lit a lamp in the shed, and it was by this glow that he helped the fool climb down the ladder into the sewer

pipe. The bottom of the concrete pipe was damp. After crawling only a short way, he heard some rumbling above him. He
stopped, frightened, for he was now almost totally in the
blackness. The Pole's sack slipped off his shoulders into a pool
of water. It was becoming difficult to breathe. "Go on," he
heard echoing from the driver's end of the pipe. "There's
nothin' to be frightened of."

Tadeusz pulled himself along by grabbing on to some metal
rungs fastened into the side of the pipe. When he could hardly
distinguish the driver's voice or Polish song from the loud
dripping anymore, when the sewer dipped a little to the left
and met another pipe that ran directly upward, Chaim was
certain he heard some voices yelling in Yiddish from several
small sewer covers less than two meters above his head. He
gagged, then coughed when something dripped from the roof
of the pipe onto his forehead, "Someone comes," he heard.
"Pull the cover, quick!"

"I'm here, mister," someone called in accented Polish at the
far end of the pipe. "I'm here for you."

With the aid of the thin crescent of light the Jew made by
sliding the hatch a few inches to the side, Chaim found the
slippery metal ladder that led up to the hatch.

"Hurry, mister," the voice said. "Give us the food."

Two hands pushed through the narrow opening and
grabbed for the garbage Chaim Turkow was pushing upward.
But just as the last part of the driver's sack was pulled free,
the hands disappeared and the hatch cover was almost pushed
back into place, leaving only a small opening to one side.

"Wait, wait," Chaim was told.

Perhaps only a fool, a Jewish fool, would have done what
Chaim did next — but there was no choice, was there? He had

to see something. He climbed higher up the ladder, and after reaching the edge of the cover, he pushed as hard as he could. The cover shifted slightly to the left, allowing enough space for Chaim to raise his eyes over the edge of the filthy opening.

The one who took the driver's food into the new country of the Jews sat by the sewer, where he divided the vegetables and crusts of bread into smaller sacks. Two others with blackened faces stuffed these sacks into their jackets, and then, from behind the sewer cover, a woman with her own bundle came into view. "Please, Yakov," she begged one of them. "I won't ask again."

By twisting his body around the slippery ladder, Chaim saw this Yakov take a piece of bread from his sack and give it to the woman. She quickly chewed the bread, spat it into her hand, and when she removed the bundle of rags from her back, pushed her hand into an opening at the top of the bundle. "Take, take," she said. If the woman hadn't moved to within inches of the sewer with her hand held out for another crust, Chaim Turkow wouldn't have heard the bundle cry for a second, then cough.

Chaim's hands were already raw from gripping the ladder. He tried to move even farther around the lip of the opening, and when he slipped off one of the rungs, he reached for some wires that were hanging from the top of the sewer wall. The wire — who knows, maybe it once carried phone conversations from one end of Warsaw to the other — steadied him for a second on the ladder again before it broke away from the wall.

"Hey, boy," the driver called from the other end of the world. "What's takin' you so long? Boy!"

To the accompaniment of the Pole's cries, our Turkow low-

ered himself to the bottom of the sewer. His chest heaved.
He gagged. "Take, take," he said when he regained some
breath, and then, working under the thin bead of light that
still shone through from above, he shaped the wire — first
came the trunk, next the arms. The head was easier. "Hold
your breath, steady your balance," he muttered, as Milutsky
might have said to any nervous artist. "Everything takes time."

He felt the shape of the wire figure — no larger than his
fist — bending smoothly as he handled it. His hand bled,
pricked by one of the sharp ends, but he had to keep pushing
the wire into his palm. "Take, take."

Like a piece of clay that finds a form no matter what we do,
the small wire figure was imperfect: the arms were too long,
the head too large for the trunk. He scraped some mud off the
sewer wall and worked it into the figure's arms.

Chaim worked until the Jew above him dropped his hand
through the opening with payment due the Pole.

"That's all we have today," the voice said. "Bring whatever
you can tomorrow."

It might have meant the end of everything for the fool holding on to the ladder, but Chaim Turkow pulled himself up
the ladder before the Jew disappeared. He squeezed the hand
and pushed the wire figure through the sewer opening. "For
the woman," Chaim said in Yiddish. "This is for the woman
with the bundle."

12

SLIGHTLY THINNER and a bit paler, Witold Grunewald celebrated his return to the estate of his ancestors by purchasing a case of champagne for himself, a strand of pearls for Frau Grunewald, and a shimmering blue-green dress for his mournful daughter. For the servants he had a basketful of pastries and white breads covered by packets of black-market sugar. "Sweets for everyone," he announced at his own front door when his household staff drew up before him like supplicants. "I am home at last."

There followed the usual hugs and embraces as well as Herr Grunewald's extensive list of complaints: that Warsaw was a shambles, with drunkards, prostitutes, and sallow-faced priests on every corner; that one had to be careful of thieving shop-owners (Herr Grunewald almost said "Jew" before "shop-owners," but caught himself and smiled); that a good meal was almost impossible to find, even at the best hotels used by the officers; and that a certain Roman Ratynski, "hired as a team-ster for a very good wage," deserted him while he struggled with his bowels in a lice-ridden public lavatory. Pouring the wine into goblets, Herr Grunewald jingled one of his full purses for his wife. "And the smells from certain sections," he added while the good Frau gingerly rolled the pearls in her hands, "are simply horrible."

Herr Grunewald slipped the beautiful strand of pearls around his wife's smooth neck.

"But it's been hard for us, too, Witold," she complained. There was the constant pilfering of their larder by the servants, the continuing moodiness of Fräulein Grunewald, the dreadful game meat Elzbieta was getting from the peasants, the explosions and bright flashes that kept her awake at night. Worst of all, she couldn't forget that awful afternoon when the soldiers punished some Polish partisans at the edge of the Grunewald estate. But when Witold asked her what, exactly, she meant by punishment, his wife said it was "too much" for her to say, at least until she finished the wine.

"I stayed inside for three days until Elzbieta told me it was all over. She said something about a tree and a girl and how hard the earth was. You know how the old woman babbles in that mountain dialect of hers. A young German officer told me he was getting rid of a few partisans, so we had tea and I told him that I, too, loved the Reich but I didn't wish to see whatever it was he intended to do. 'Don't trouble yourself, Frau,' he answered. 'We deal with these troubles all the time.' Then we had our tea and schnapps and he told me all about his father's leather shop in Bremen."

Unnoticed by the Grunewalds, Chaim Turkow stood in the darkest corner of the now-rugless sitting room and shuffled his feet in a layer of dust. He chewed on his quarter-loaf of white bread and licked his allotment of sugar. With Frau Grunewald's expensive Persian carpets and silk tapestries well on their way to the homes of various German officers, and the crystal chandelier from Moravia already installed in a Wehrmacht spa in Karlsbad, the sitting room was nearly bare.

Witold held his wife's hand while she spoke. "How we suffered," she said. "When they brought some wounded soldiers by the house in those ambulances, they demanded we cut up some of our best linen for fresh bandages!" Of course, the Frau continued, living under such hardship did help their daughter cope with her grief. "Every day, the dearest wore her best dress and stood by the gate with brandy-water and those little cakes Elzbieta still makes for us."

Herr Grunewald gasped, then recovered enough breath to praise such patriotic concern. It wouldn't do, he thought, to mention the real state of affairs in the east or to tell his Frau some of the stories he'd heard from other officers in the Hotel Europejski's expensive bordello. After all, delicacy (and the Frau's sanity in these empty rooms) required a blank mind and a slight hope for the future — a hope that would vanish if Herr Grunewald conjured up the stories about the festering stumps or yellow burn blisters of Panzer group leaders who sought a good Polish fuck to ease their pain. No, it wouldn't do at all.

Instead, he turned to the subject of their coming move to Sweden. "Think of what you'll be able to buy, my love," he said as Frau Grunewald wiped her face. "Those Swedes have hoarded everything we need."

No doubt about it — Herr Grunewald had struck just the right chord with his wife. He told her how much money he had and how well they would live, and then, because he wanted to make his wife laugh, Herr Grunewald got up from the couch and did a very funny reenactment of the moment when his Warsaw driver, as green as Baltic seawater, came running back to his truck with the fool in tow ("He smelled like he'd helped the Polack with his stomach problems!"), apologizing for his abominable act of leaving "the great Pan Grunowski" to guard the crates by himself. " 'Ohh, sir, sir, my ass was as raw as a wound,' " Witold whined in Polish.

" 'Bad sausage, bad drink, made me go home for a little salve.' "

Propping himself by the door, Herr Grunewald — with as much devotion and energy to his craft as any good cabaret dunce in Berlin — continued to entertain Frau Grunewald with the sad story of the girl in the convent. " 'Scandal of scandals,' " he roared like the Mother Superior, " 'your parts are leaking over my Lord and husband's clean floor.' "

Timing was everything, and Witold Grunewald knew he'd prepared his wife well for what was coming. "No more, no more," she gasped, laughing, as she slid off the couch to the floor. "My chest will break open any second!"

"But please don't let that happen until we leave for Sweden. We now have, you see, enough money for a safe passage."

"When, Witold?"

"Soon. I'll send a few cables to get our papers straightened out — but let's have a little champagne and think about replacing everything you've given up. Once we get to Stockholm, no more talk of this swinish place."

Showman that he was, Herr Grunwald let the proof of his intent spill out of a dozen velvet bags he pulled from his valise.

"Clinkety, clink, dearest . . . all the way to Stockholm's best shopping district."

Frau Grunewald was astonished. She picked up the shiny pieces of gold — some in coins, most in those funny, jagged shapes that had been thoroughly cleaned by expert jewelers — and bounced a handful of this solid weight in front of her husband. "So much?"

"Ah, dearest, our German brothers did love your good taste in furnishings and art."

Then Herr Grunewald, happy to see his good wife dazzled

by this display, praised the glory of his champagne by helping himself to a third glass.

Frau Grunewald finally took notice of the fool in the corner who picked at this bread and dropped crumbs on the floor. "Find Elzbieta, Tadek," she said. "She'll see to your meal and" — a quick look to Witold — "go through a few beads with you in the kitchen."

Chaim pretended he didn't know where he was and stuffed the remaining portion of bread into his cheeks. If thoughts of Stockholm, new china, silver, and soft rugs hadn't so pre-occupied his mistress, she probably would have disciplined the Polack for making a mess in her sitting room — but Frau Grunewald, wrapped in pearls and a bit excited by her husband's hand, ignored the Pole's crude manners and instead slipped a finger into Witold Grunewald's open shirt.

"When? Tell me when," she moaned close to his breast.

"Clinkety, clink, clink, clink."

✦ ✦ ✦

Because the breezes had become unseasonably warm, Elzbieta said her prayers with her head thrust out the kitchen window, which faced in the general direction of the Black Madonna's spiritual home. The three hundred miles separating her from the angelic face of Poland's treasure in Czestochowa meant nothing to her. "She knows I'm here, Tadek, loving her every second." And while Chaim sipped the hot broth she prepared just for him, the old woman genuflected between her stove and the blessed western window. "The bad times are coming," she repeated in her thick accent. "Help me to understand, Holy Mother. Help this poor boy too."

Chaim Turkow blew into a fat globule of grease that

skimmed the surface of his soup. The photographs and sketches pressed against his chest between two layers of cotton cloth. He ate the soup. When the cook eyed him from the window, he dutifully crossed himself as she expected.

"We were very cold this winter, Tadek. Every day we waited for you to come back. The girls paid no attention to the mistress and they stole food from my larder. Right in front of me, they did this! 'Put that back,' I'd say. 'What right have you to take whatever you want? You should wait until we know they're dead on the road before you borrow anything. A sin is a sin, even if we hate the master.'"

Elzbieta twisted the rosary into her torn shawl.

"As She is my witness, I told them every day what the priest said before he ran away from the village. Always the same: 'Put that back until we know they're dead. A sin is a sin.' Still they don't care for nothing but to open their fat legs for the village boys who sniff around here looking for their dirty smells and my cakes. I've seen a few of them lying in the barn with these boys where they grunt off their sweat on top of each other."

The fool watched the old woman's hands mold a piece of bread. He crossed himself and moaned. Elzbieta closed the window and the door.

"A few weeks ago there was shooting all night," Elzbieta said to the beautiful man who looked a bit sick despite her soup and the soft bread. "I heard them prowling in the woods, shooting to scare the partisans away. They caught Jacek, the skinny one from the village who used to help his father shoe our horses and stick medicines up their arses. He didn't wear his cap when the soldiers dragged him by his feet past our gate.

"A big German with a red face says to me as he comes past

my window, 'Look closely and see your comrade, Pani.' Right from that window over there, I can see them kicking at Jacek's head — and all the boy wanted was his cap and a chance to see his father before they took him to the tree with the others they'd caught."

For a moment Elzbieta shut her eyes and held her fool's hand. She ate a bit of his soup, but left the few chunks of stringy meat for Tadeusz.

"The red face signals to the truck parked by our gate — 'Oh, ah,' he yells to the other soldiers. 'Let's be done with this.' That's when I see the five from the village tied together.

"First they hanged Bogdan the farmer, then came Andrzej, who crapped all over himself when his rope was tied to the limb. Next they did it to Artur and his cousin, Franiek, and then when the men and boys were swinging, a few soldiers smashed their faces with rifles in front of the girl, Joanna — the pretty one who used to work for chemist Rokita — well, she had to watch this because she was last in the line to hear Red Face read from a paper in his bad Polish. Two of our house girls here come running to stand with me, and when they want to hide, I take their arms so they won't think about stealing groats or a little flour when such things as this go on. 'Don't you forget this,' I told them. 'Don't you ever forget how they turned faces into jelly at Grunewald's great birch tree!'

"The German red face made all of us march past. Well, not everyone. Frau Grunewald got to stay inside because she was sick and not one of us. 'Jelly,' I whispered to Izabela. 'Think of them this way.'

"The girl Joanna was still alive when we walked to see them. Her eyes bulged, but she was getting a little air because the rope wasn't tight enough. 'Pigs to pigs,' Red Face laughed."

Back at her window, Elzbieta motioned for Tadeusz to look at the tree Herr Grunewald's grandfather planted to celebrate a good harvest. The bright sunlight made the cook wince and turn away from the window and close the kitchen door. She whispered to him that she'd heard gossip that, before the moon was full in two days, a band of Soviet partisans from the forests would take their revenge on the *Volksdeutscher* they held accountable for the deaths of the villagers.

Elzbieta took the fool's hand. "You come with me, Tadek, to see where I buried Joanna."

Not far from Witold Grunewald's apple orchard, a hundred or so meters from the house, Elzbieta brushed away some leaves from a mound of dirt. She told Tadeusz how the red face cut down the men and left the girl swinging for the women on the estate to see. "No one cared but me . . . I cut the rope and yelled out to the Virgin to tell me what to do. 'A white sheet,' I know she told me. 'Make a fire and soften the ground for this girl of mine.' "

It started to drizzle. Elzbieta found a branch and dug a narrow trench from the highest point of Joanna's grave to a spot some ten meters away.

Chaim went to help her, but she pushed him off. "I will do this myself so she should have a little dry peace."

For all the good it did when the drizzle turned into a downpour, Chaim took off his cap and held it above the old woman's head. Elzbieta looked at him and saw the lines forming under his blue eyes and the patchy stubble of blond whiskers above his lips. The boy Tadek was now covered by the pale shell of a Polish man.

"No one knows," she mumbled, seeing how tall and stooped over he'd become, "how the devil works if he sets his mind to things."

With his beret stuck to her head like a postage stamp, Elzbieta told this fool who lost his voice so long ago not to be frightened about the full moon. "On Mary's grave," she made him promise by placing his hand on her chest and making the sign of the cross. "On Her virgin heart too."

When the rain stopped, the old woman ran back to the house and left the fool to think about what had happened. Chaim waited by the grave for several hours. He tried to build up the mound a bit by placing stones at each end, and then he straightened the crude wooden cross Elzbieta had nailed together from scraps she'd found at his hut. He thought about praying for the girl.

Given these circumstances, how could Chaim Turkow have known that only fifty kilometers away from Herr Grunewald's estate, the soldiers Witold Grunewald had once entertained on his green lawn were suffocating under the bodies of young Panzer grenadiers who, abandoning their burning tanks, had exploded into splinters and fat when a direct Soviet hit skipped over their three tanks and plopped into their dwindling store of petrol? These young bodies, or what was left of them, flew backward with such force into Herr Grunewald's former guests — despite conditions, they were drinking ersatz coffee and laughing — that each was cut by a dozen missiles of molten shrapnel.

And certainly Chaim Turkow couldn't have known how Anya Kravitz, who left the good sisters in Warsaw with her vegetable basket one day and wandered near one of the deeper scratches on her arm, was now pulling at her throat inside a well-designed chamber with two hundred other Jewish women and a few infants in the lush countryside not far from where Kopernik himself first mapped out a reasonable plan for understanding God's amazing universe.

So we ask for your understanding. How could Chaim Turkow have known any of this when he finally clutched at his pocket and realized that his photographs and sketches were soaked through? And had he not fallen on the girl's grave, tearing at his coat and screaming out curses in Yiddish, a Soviet captain named Glibshin, who was waiting in some bushes about fifty meters away from the Jew, might never have chosen that second to give his men permission to fire their mortar shells into the large home he suspected was sheltering a band of reactionary collaborators or German soldiers.

"Show them we're here, boys," Captain Glibshin shouted. "Remember who they are!"

And Mikhail Glibshin's men always followed their orders — even if they came from the mouth of a Leningrad Jew-captain who wore Stalin's Red Star.

"Now," the captain ordered while he watched the strange-looking Jew by the grave scream again. "Now!"

13

IF LEYZER ERLICH ever visited Nowy Dwor, he would
have elicited from the Jews in Moishe Turkow's inn (the
rabbi included) the same response he received from the
Jews in Lodz, Bialystok, Stanislaw, Kovel, and a hundred other
places when, always following the conclusion of Shabbos,
Leyzer stood in the middle of some dusty market square and
made five small bananas appear from behind his dog's ears.
The trick never ceased to amaze Poles and Jews, and everyone
cheered when the dwarf said to his ugly cur, "Here, Poozie,
give *mein Kinder* some beautiful fruit."

Without stopping for a breath, Leyzer Erlich would bow to
the dog, peel back the smooth, yellow skin of the mysterious
fruit few had ever seen before, and, snapping his fingers as he
bit off the top of the fruit, walk into the crowd and proceed
to pull out colored strings from the yarmulkes of open-mouthed
yeshiva boys, oranges (oranges!) from his own pair of tiny
boots, and — the trick of all tricks — a cooing dove that somehow found its way into one of the velvet tallith bags of a
respectable elder. "Ahh," they said as they moved closer to
this strange dwarf (if you could lay Leyzer out end-to-end, he
measured no more than one meter plus a baby's finger) —
"Ahh!"

No doubt about it: from town to town throughout Poland, the Ukraine, and Byelorussia, Leyzer Erlich had for thirty years been closing out the day of rest and unhinging Jewish mouths with spectacular tricks. He said he knew a thousand tricks — "It would take me a lifetime to perform all I can do" — and even the poorest *shtetl* Jew or peasant found at least a single coin to contribute to this little man's well-being. People fought over the honor of inviting him to spend the night with them, and when he accepted such an invitation (he liked to stay with anyone who had children), he always treated his host to his knowledge of esoteric Talmudic arguments, Hasidic tales, and even stories about the great Polish kings. "A thousand tricks, a thousand stories, mean a certain return," he'd promise before he left in the morning. "Leyzer Erlich always comes back!"

Leyzer spoke several languages besides Yiddish and Polish — Ukrainian, German, enough Lithuanian to make people believe he'd studied in Vilna all his life, mountain dialects that sounded like coughing to the Jews of Warsaw or Krakow. He knew phrasebook English and some unusual French verbs, and, of course, had a passing acquaintance with Byelorussian. After twenty years of travel across borders (easily traversed without documents when one can, as Leyzer invariably did, perform the banana trick for astounded customs officials and surly border policemen), Leyzer Erlich had used up three Poozies and maybe a tenth of his stories and tricks. No matter where he found himself, this little Jew, who often carried his dog in a sack, delighted both pogromist and Jew alike — even, as it would happen, in Gehenna itself.

When the blood brothers of Herr Grunewald came to Poland during the reign of Poozie IV, Leyzer Erlich had just finished a two-week stay in Zabno. His legs were weakened from performing in front of a large crowd of Jews who, despite the war scares of the previous month, continued about their daily business. The three hundred or so faithful souls who applauded his wonderful tricks demanded he remain with them if conditions became dangerous.

"What's a week, more or less?" the richest merchant in the town asked Leyzer. "These things blow over like a bad wind." When the merchant — his name was Y. K. Wawelberg, a grain wholesaler — offered the tired magician free board and room and, most attractive of all, a splendid gold-leafed volume of essays by the Rebbe of Gur, Leyzer changed his plans. "I'll stay," he said. "My ankles feel like ripe melons about to burst."

Well, you know the story after this: Zabno was sucked into the whirlwind. Unlike the people of Nowy Dwor, the citizens of Zabno lasted all of seven days because an overzealous German officer misunderstood his orders, lined up every Jew he could find (an easy task in such a small place), and locked them inside Y. K. Wawelberg's huge grain storehouse. Over the course of this one week in mid-September, Zabno's Jews, led by the well-dressed Y. K. Wawelberg himself, were forced to bag every morsel of grain. Before sunset on Friday the rabbi told his Jews to stop working, as Shabbos was at hand. The officer who supervised this important work was forced to make a decision on the spot: "Finish," he yelled through the doorway of the storehouse, "before I count to ten."

The rabbi, his beard turning white in front of many of his best pupils, explained to the officer that all work would be completed as soon as the sabbath passed.

"Three, four," the officer continued, oblivious to the pleas of the rabbi and even Y. K. Wawelberg (who spoke excellent German). "Five, six . . ."

The officer's slow count was accompanied by his soldiers' preparations: torches were set ablaze, smoke wafted into the windows as privates and corporals positioned themselves at each of the four corners of Wawelberg's storehouse. Yes, there was crying and screaming and pleading.

"Seven, eight . . ."

And yes, there was Leyzer Erlich, finally, heaving banana after banana outside at the feet of the calm officer.

"Send the dwarf to me," the officer shouted, interrupting his count at nine. "Now!"

The magician was passed over the heads of the tallest Jews and pushed through an air vent. Still producing fruit from somewhere (he was down to cherries), Leyzer politely greeted the officer in German.

"Where did you get the fruit?" the officer asked. (He'd once developed a taste for the exotic when he worked as a clerk for a Bavarian shipping company in East Africa.)

Leyzer Erlich shrugged his miniature shoulders and showered the German with at least a dozen more cherries and a five-meter length of colored cloth pulled from the officer's leather map case, and while he, Leyzer, pretended to swat at a pesky horsefly, he distracted the officer enough to produce a small music box that played the same German lullaby that the officer loved to sing to his daughter.

The counting stopped. The officer and his men gathered around Leyzer Erlich. Poozie nipped her way into the circle and spun, flipped over twice (many cheers), and sat on her haunches with a tin cup between her yellowed teeth. "Contributions are always welcome, *mein Herr*," Leyzer said with a smile. "Ten marks or the safety of these people, who merely wish to sit down lest they offend their God."

After such a hard slog through Poland, the German officer forgot about the grainhouse Jews when he saw Leyzer Erlich make something out of nothing. The torches were put out, the Jews collapsed onto in a heap (still crying and yelling) — and because he promised the Germans a fine show with many more tricks, Leyzer Erlich bought the Jews of Zabno twenty-four hours of sabbath peace.

That night Leyzer and Poozie were given very good quality soup and tinned beef. The officer and his men were entertained with tricks, jokes, and stories while they sat in the spacious dining room of the absent Y. K. Wawelberg. By late afternoon of the next day, the officer agreed to keep the tiny Jew as a special pet. If you can make some cherries or bananas from nothing for the Wehrmacht, you can bargain with anyone, and so Leyzer said that unless he was assured the Jews of Zabno would come to no harm, he was certain his magician's hands would cramp and tighten and thus prevent him from performing for anyone. "Agreed," the officer said with a chuckle. "All we want is their cooperation."

Leyzer and Poozie were loaded into the back of a large army truck (along with five or six sacks containing Reb Wawelberg's books and precious stamp collection) and driven out of Zabno an hour before Shabbos ended. While Leyzer Erlich rehearsed some German songs with Poozie as they bounced over potholes, while the officer played his lullaby over and over again, the torches were at last thrown through the windows of Y. K. Wawelberg's granary.

But magic can last only so long. After a few months, trucks are needed for more important duties, and a Jew-dwarf, no matter how much pleasure he brings, becomes expendable. The officer became the administrator of a small camp in central Poland destined by the lawyers and doctors of philosophy in Berlin to become an even larger camp once the grand plan was set into motion. "For tricks, you get time," the new commandant told Leyzer. "My word is my compact." Leyzer pledged his loyalty (was there a choice?) and was assigned a daytime job in the camp's primitive infirmary after proving himself again and again (though Poozie died when she ate some spoiled ham), and while so many others vanished, the dwarf became a master of life who joked with the Jewish children as they began to follow their parents to the concrete bunkers that German ingenuity had built close to a birch wood. He often thought about killing himself, but how could he let children go to the wood without a tender word, a bit of a story, a wave? Life, you see, became Leyzer Erlich's greatest feat. I will outlive them, he promised himself. No matter what happens, *I will outlive them!*

Five years after Leyzer pledged himself to continuous breathing, he was still in the same camp, though he made frequent visits to other places where his efficient and respected officer was busily engaged in advising his colleagues. The fruit appeared less often, but Leyzer Erlich could always turn to his colored cloth, bits of thin metal that he shaped into tin soldiers, or shredded newspapers that became roses at the snap of his fingers. Sometimes he turned an apple into an orange, but the machine that was too enormous to swallow a dwarf never stopped: children continued to alight from the cattlecars, old people arrived from as far away as Yugoslavia and Greece, uniformed doctors who stationed themselves at the platform's edge kept pointing their silver-tipped sticks toward the birch wood and the dense smoke. Leyzer Erlich told his jokes in five languages and counted the days and the Jews; and he was certain he was even shorter than before.

✦ ✦ ✦

When Frau Grunewald first saw those blazing lights streak across the sky, Leyzer Erlich — a hundred kilometers to the south — was left without a single banana. It didn't matter, either, for there wasn't anyone around to swoon and beg for more from the dwarf. The Germans were gone.

The officers fled with their men, leaving behind mountains of expertly kept records and ledgers, bent spectacles, valises, and children's frocks. By hiding inside a still-warm baker's oven with a Jehovah's Witness and a Polish surgeon from Lodz, Leyzer waited without water or much air until he heard the clankety-clank sound made by Russian tanks. Covered by soot and crusts of burnt bread, Leyzer Erlich popped out of his oven the moment he heard a Russian boot kick against the wrought-iron door. "Greetings, comrade," he announced in Russian to the startled Soviet rifleman. "You want to suck on an orange?"

Then, for the first time in years, Leyzer Erlich wept without stopping, unable to produce the promised orange or much else except some thick phlegm from being in the oven and, after the coughing stopped, the last few words of the Jehovah's Witness. The rifleman put the dwarf from the oven on a cart and gave him a drink of water that stank from the smell of the camp.

"I'll get my officer," he told Leyzer. "You are free." Leyzer demanded to speak to the highest-ranking officer, and once a major could be found, the magician began to shout out the names of thousands of children from as far away as Dubrovnik

and some hard-to-pronounce places in the Carpathian Mountains. No one tried to stop the dwarf's naming — once again,
Leyzer Erlich had found his audience.

✦ ✦ ✦

Who else, then, but a tiny Jew now traveling with the Red
Army in its first operations into Poland would have known how
to approach the young man with the blue eyes and blond hair
who sat, feet splayed out, head bandaged, murmuring in
Yiddish? Who else would have known exactly what to do
when a Soviet captain demanded to know why this strange-
looking Jew was hiding near a house whose occupants were
known fascists?

"The colonel wants us to shoot him," a Soviet captain named
Glibshin said. "And if he doesn't talk sense, I don't think I'll
be able to stop it. Two times he fell into the fire, and once he
nearly jabbed a fork into his eyes. See what you can do,
Comrade Erlich. A Jew can be guilty, too."

First, Leyzer Erlich learned the blond Jew's name and town;
next, and by far the most difficult assignment, he had to convince this man who wanted to hurt himself that he, Chaim
Turkow from Nowy Dwor, was safe.

"They say you worked for the *Volksdeutscher* pig, brother.
True?"

No response.

"They say the dead Poles they found in the house were all
members of a gang of fascist bandits. True?"

More silence.

"They say many things, my brother, and to be quite blunt
with you, unless you're willing to throw away your fears and
speak the truth, no one — not even that Jewish captain who

kept his men from pumping a pistol shot into your neck — not even he can help you anymore. These goyim are as serious as the ones they've pushed back into Germany!"

Chaim Turkow twisted against the rope that bound his wrists. He looked at the dwarf, and, just before he was sick over himself, asked the only question that mattered. "Where are they, please? Where have they all gone?"

Leyzer Erlich worked his own tiny fingers inside the man's clenched palms. "There can't be any more illusions, brother," he began. "It's like this, you see — I came to Zabno to make some tricks and earn a few zloty. In the autumn, it was. In '39 . . ."

Halfway through Leyzer Erlich's story — the same one we told you — Captain Glibshin and his superior officer, a pock-faced colonel who had better things to do with his time, opened the tent flap and demanded to listen to "the interrogation."

"Comrade Colonel," said Leyzer. "My Russian is not up to your standard, so you'll forgive me if I continue telling this Jew about myself in our own language. If I judge my brother here correctly, I'll soon find out why he was hiding in the fascist's woods."

"No tricks." The colonel rolled a Turkish cigarette. "This isn't a fool's performance."

On his own diminished authority, Leyzer untied the Jew's hands. He positioned himself between Chaim and the officers and took this Jew into the blackness. *Everything* was named; the numbers counted and memorized by a dwarf infirmary attendant were expressed. Leyzer Erlich rattled off the names of town after town that turned his camp into a final resting place for anyone who ever celebrated the High Holy Days or made jokes about a rabbi's wife.

"Some sang at the end," he remembered, describing how he stood by the window of the camp infirmary and pressed his ears against the glass ("To make the sounds louder, gentlemen. To make them like arrows into my soft brain . . ."). "Most cried. A few danced."

He told this blond Jew about the night he twirled like a top in front of the Germans and Lithuanian SS guards, just the way Poozie used to when she wanted attention — this time, however, the dog was a man and the audience had just finished a hard two weeks' worth of work disposing of twenty thousand Hungarians. And the puppet show he staged for the officers' children in the commandant's parlor (two banana tricks, one orange, and, for an encore, lots of Poozie rolls and yelps; cakes for the nice children, a chicken carcass for Leyzer).

Telling his story twice — once in Yiddish for Chaim Turkow, in quick Russian translation for the two Soviet officers (Glibshin understood both versions!) — Leyzer never once let his voice waver or fail. The colonel took notes on yellow paper; Captain Glibshin stared at the ground.

Leyzer was a diary come to life, and no event was out of order. In October of '42, Gypsies parked their caravans by the front gate of the camp. "Is this where we rest?" their leader asked a smiling guard. "We were promised work and blankets, sir." Unable to resist lapsing into German for a second, Leyzer gave the young soldier's answer: *"Ja, ja, mein Wagenführer, hier ist die Stelle."*

"They didn't make them undress, either," Leyzer added. "They went to the wood, clothes and all. A *first* for our camp!"

Not too long after the Gypsies came and went, the Kapos wisely lost a soccer match to the Ukrainian guards on the day when twenty-five boxcars arrived loaded with Dutch Jews, dressed in their best suits, their children well behaved and orderly and carrying little sacks filled with jams and sweets they brought from Rotterdam's lovely shops. The job took only three hours because everyone was so cooperative and mindful of the rules. Leyzer counted off the hours in Yiddish and Russian. Three hours exactly.

The colonel interrupted. *"Three,* comrade?"

"Three."

"And what was it the German said to the Gypsy?"

"He said, Comrade Colonel, 'This *is* the place.' "

Leyzer was as animated as the late Poozie in the throes of a leap and rollover.

"Yes, Colonel — in only three hours it's possible to do almost anything. Let me show you how it worked."

His short legs churning up and down like pistons, the dwarf rushed about the tent.

"Here is a fine Jew, say, from Amsterdam. He brushes his coat because he's never been so close to so many unwashed people before. And *this smell* that clings to his coat — whew, awful! Brush, brush, brush and it's still there. Well, what's he to do about that, eh?

"Look at him, gentlemen: our fine middle-aged Dutch Jew, a Latin teacher, say, who never got to finish telling his eager charges about Livy or whatever it was that Caesar did in Gaul.

"Here he is . . . brush, brush, brush . . . on the concrete platform along with families he's seen all his life: the doctor from the polyclinic is over there squashed between two other yellow stars, holding his black bag — our doctor was told his services would be necessary once everyone got settled in the labor camp — and there's the salted-fish exporter who liked to

collect those early Rembrandt prints. Hello, doctor, what a
mess we're in, yes? No, wait, who else does he see? Why, it's
his neighbor, the seller of the candied fruits all Amsterdam
loved during the holiday season. Must speak to him as soon
as this sorting-out business is over and done with, our Latinist thinks. A smart man, our candy merchant — and a sup-
porter of the classics in our Jewish school. I'll speak to him
later!

"Wives and children, former and present students are all
here. Dresses are smoothed down; ties are straightened and
knotted in the correct way now that one can breathe a little
away from these hollow-looking *Ostjuden*. Glances are exchanged; eyebrows dance the signal. 'Yes, I am here. An awful
journey, but at least we can settle down to business now and
wait until the Germans are taught a proper lesson by the
Allies.' "

The major stopped writing. After all, this little Jew's antics
required attention. Proper Intelligence thrived, he knew, on
bits and pieces: this *he'd* learned as a young lieutenant dealing
with the traitors Comrade Stalin exposed after '35.

"Brush, brush, brush. 'Keep them quiet, dear Rosa . . . make
Stefan stop whining so. It gives a bad impression.'

"Brush, brush, brush.

" 'Ah, you see, the line is moving along. Where are they
taking our bags? Should I tell them to mind the large brown
one with the rope? Those Polish porters couldn't tell the
difference between a good piece of luggage and a crate of
herring. Careful or no tip, you!

" 'My age? Forty-nine this December, sir. Occupation?
Senior lecturer in classics at the Wilhelmina Gymnasium, with
additional duties in German and French. Do you know where

my family is, sir, for I seem to have lost sight of them in all of this confusion? No, no, I'm just a bit fatigued by the trip from Holland. I have no problems with my lungs. Whoosh . . . the air passes through easily when I am not so tired. Yes, of course: move to the right and join my wife and children on the stone path. I agree, *Herr Doktor*, everything will be much better after we clean ourselves. Yes, I see them now. But what about my bags? Yes, I understand — we pick them up outside the family barracks once we've washed away the journey's dust. My wife is over there, *Herr Doktor. Danke.* I will obey all the rules.

" 'Wait, Rosa. Wait for me. I'm here.' "

Transformed into this proper Dutch Jew, Leyzer ambled from one end of the tent to the other. He pretended to lift up one of the teacher's children, stroking the air where a head might have been perched against a shoulder, speaking softly to this child — boy or girl? — who undoubtedly was asking when he would have something to eat.

Just a few more steps and Leyzer the Dutchman was next to Captain Glibshin. " 'Here we are, Rosa. Undress the children and forget your modesty. This is what happens when there are so many in one group. Hurry! They're waving us in. Do remember to tie their shoelaces together. Why isn't this better organized? The children are hungry.' "

Leyzer Erlich drew back the tent flaps and stepped outside. He was still mumbling to his imaginary family — oh, you know, the sorts of things one says to a son or daughter who is frightened by all the people and the crowding.

"Whoosh. Whoosh, Chaim Turkow. Then it was over."

The colonel returned to his notepad. He numbered along the edge of his paper each of the stages acted out by the Jew, underlining the year and the people. *"Dutch in '42,"* he wrote. "Three hours."

"The names of other collaborators in the area, Comrade Erlich," Glibshin said. "Ask him about them and also these . . ."

Captain Glibshin held up a few torn sketches and the water-soaked photographs.

"Who are these people?" he asked. "Friends of the people in the house? Do they live in the village?"

Maybe Leyzer Erlich really believed he could do anything. Maybe he always knew what to do next.

"Comrades, leave the tent for a moment. I just need a moment."

The colonel extended one finger above his clenched fist. Yes, one moment.

"Chaim Turkow," Leyzer said as soon as they were alone. "I need to know enough to tell them something. The Russians — even that Jewish captain who saved you only because he heard your Yiddish — are suspicious of everything and everyone. Lie if you must, but say something."

"What was the 'whoosh'?"

"The end of the Dutchman, brother."

"And the others?"

"Yes."

"Poles?"

"Poles and Russians in the beginning, for the first year. Then French, Germans, the Dutch, Slovenes, Czechs, Serbians, Italians, a flood of Hungarians in '44."

Leyzer put his hands behind his back and found an apple.

"Here, you see this little globe? This is where we are, right where my finger cuts into the skin. This is Poland. I pull the skin off. Whoosh . . . everyone!"

"Give me a knife, magician," Chaim Turkow begged in a whisper.

"You want this knife to help you join your people from the Narew?"

Chaim nodded.

"Then watch my forehead, Chaim Turkow. This is a better trick."

As Chaim shifted in his chair, Leyzer Erlich threw himself at the Jew, scratching and pounding him across the face. The two officers rushed into the tent and tried to pull the little man from his enemy, but he stuck to the prisoner like an insect drawn to sugar — he punched, slapped, and dug his fingernails into Chaim's throat. Glibshin yanked Leyzer's feet. "Enough, we'll deal with him."

More punches. Some biting. Finally, his hands bruised from his last slap at Chaim, Leyzer Erlich let himself be dragged away by the colonel, who, now certain the dwarf knew a real spy when he saw one, took his pistol and pointed it at the back of Chaim Turkow's blond head.

"No!" Leyzer screamed. "Can't you see what he is?"

The colonel told the magician not to look.

Leyzer crawled between the captain's legs, reaching Chaim Turkow's bleeding face before the colonel's pistol received its bullet from the magazine. He grabbed the photographs and sketches from Chaim and threw them in from of the colonel. He also prayed he was right.

"Comrade," Leyzer said, "this man is a great artist, known throughout Jewish Poland. And if you look at the pictures you'll see all that is left of him."

The colonel picked up the sketches and walked over to the kerosene lantern. He turned up the light.

Leyzer continued to plead. "This is no spy, comrades. Here we have a man of passion. A useful man, gentlemen. A man who knows how to use a camera *and* a brush."

"Are these your people?" Glibshin asked in Yiddish. "Is the magician right?"

"Yes," Chaim said. "I've lost all of them."

"And this photo we found was taken where?"

"In Nowy Dwor — in the beginning."

Captain Glibshin turned to Leyzer. "What did you say to him to make him talk?"

Leyzer rose up to his full height, a diminutive guard to his brother from across the river Narew. He spoke in Yiddish to the Soviet captain. "I told him, Comrade Captain, that if he let himself be killed for his stupid silence, he would kill the dead again. Who would be left to explain those faces?"

"But you were hitting him!"

"So I talked a little in his ear, too! Who can stand a fool?"

"Dammit, Glibshin," the colonel yelled. "Translate!"

"Comrade Colonel, it's very simple: the dwarf says all this Jew wants to do is remember for us."

"Remember? Remember what?"

Chaim Turkow held up the sketch of his mother and sisters sitting on the front porch of Moishe Turkow's inn. "Tell the Russian," Chaim said to Leyzer. "Tell him the little girl holding the book was my sister Manya — tell him she taught me how to draw . . ."

Lucky guess for Leyzer Erlich!

14

JUST BEFORE the autumn rains, Leyzer Erlich began to cough up blood and, he told Chaim Turkow, pieces of the camp. Without all those numbers to remember — the colonel had written down every digit — Leyzer started to train a mangy, three-legged mongrel, bitten clean to the bone by everything that crawled. With the help of the Jew from Nowy Dwor, Leyzer fashioned a wooden paw for the new Poozie and taught the animal some basic stunts (the rollover, of course; the "find the apple behind the goy's trousers" trick, which the slightly-off-center dog learned after a bit of fattening and affection).

It didn't matter to the dwarf that the Reds laughed at the attention he paid to the dog, but he was apt to scream at the Russian intruders when they interfered with him during the most complex task of all — teaching Chaim Turkow, this artist and former idiot, how to keep the few Jewish children in Poland from going mad. "They'll need us," Leyzer said. "I know how to make them laugh, give them fruit, and soon even you will learn how to be a good enough storyteller!"

The Soviet soldiers, who sometimes hid behind trees or an armored car, watched him show Chaim Turkow how to make apples from nothing (it all involves springs) or the best way to raise his voice during a dramatic story — for Leyzer Erlich and Chaim Turkow knew how important they were to the colonel and his Yiddish-speaking captain as translators and gatherers of information.

"Bring the dwarf," the policeman-colonel would say said to Captain Glibshin. "Or if you can't find him, get the other Jew. I have someone in my tent who says he comes from . . ."

Poozie in tow, Chaim Turkow usually accompanying, Leyzer Erlich greeted another bedraggled Jew from a camp, a ghetto somewhere, someone hidden in a barn by a Pole, or, as happened seventeen times, one who crawled out from a pit.

"I'm here, brother," our magicians invariably said in Yiddish. "And I (we!) have been everywhere. Tell me what you know — I may have seen your rabbi somewhere."

Month after month they came: boys hardly out of their childhoods from Lubscza; the dozen girls liberated from a pigsty in Pinsk; a truckload of men discovered by the Soviets in an abandoned church in Wysock; and from the forests surrounding Bialystok, the frightened remnants of a Jewish partisan group. To every Jew, Leyzer gave the same introduction ("It's like this, you see. I came to Zabno to make some tricks and earn a few zloty in '39") and followed with his story about the Dutch Jew who might have been a Latinist or a doctor or a merchant and who was, always, sent to join his wife and children for a hot shower and a rest. The colonel or Captain Glibshin took notes, filling sheet after sheet of foolscap with a policeman's notation and census. "Listen to your comrade," they'd say to any terrified Jew at the appropriate moment. "It took three hours for the Dutchman — how long for those who were with you?"

"Much longer than that," said one of the boys from Lubscza. "My grandmother refused to take off her clothes for them in the forest."

"Then what happened?"

"They shot her anyway."

"And her clothes?"

"They chose me," the boy said, huddling close to one of his friends.

"Chose? For what?"

"To rip her dress off in the pit, sir. They pushed me in when it was all over and made me pull her dress off."

The officer studied the boy's pale skin, his hands. The truth was very important here. "Give me a date. Every fact is important."

Leyzer Erlich stood by the boy. "Make up a figure, brother," he whispered, "anything at all!"

"A few hours, excellency — two to march to the pit in the forest, thirty minutes to finish the job."

"But that's less than three hours — what else happened?"

"There was a lot of dirt to shovel, excellency."

The officer was impressed: nearly three hours for the Jews of Lubscza; longer for the Jews of Pinsk, who settled into their ghetto and waited for transport to labor camps "in the east"; but, try as he might, the Colonel could not get a clear answer from any of the Jewish partisans.

"We saw everything after it was over," they all agreed. "Why bother when there's nothing left?"

The amount of information kept growing because a certain dwarf wasn't able to refrain from keeping the stenographers busy with tale after tale he heard from the hundreds of Jews he interviewed. "Tell me everything," Leyzer would ask. "A Jew shouldn't ever hold anything back." and then, "everything" told, the dwarf would find one of the sallow-faced Russian women who sat at small metal tables like mindless scribes, never taking their eyes from their notebooks. "I've got an-

other story for you, Masha," the dwarf would announce. "Get
your pencil ready!"

To make matters even more complicated, this dwarf had
now gotten the one who clutched those two ruined photos to go
with him into the tents where the refugees stared at nothing
and couldn't swallow solid food.

"It's simple, Chaim — you take their hands and say, "Look,
brother, can you imagine what it was like for me?' I begin
with Zabno; for you, what you didn't know, maybe the pigs
or what happened to the butcher. It doesn't matter. Tell your
own story and then say, 'Tell me what you know!' "

Chaim listened and showed he understood, but so many
years of silence don't melt away like late spring frost, and
Leyzer Erlich began to despair over his choice of a student.
Besides, Leyzer now had blood coming from both ends, a
bodily timepiece he suspected was accurate to the minute.

The colonel soon became overwhelmed by his job. The collapse of all German resistance under the treads of Soviet
tanks throughout Poland meant, he told Glibshin, "numbers
that mount up too quickly." His soldiers brought him new
work every day: notebooks were stacked like cordwood in the
big chest he kept in his tent, and his translator — this dwarf
Jew with his many languages — took far too long to extract
useful information from these pathetic, half-dead Jews.

"Comrades," the colonel said to Leyzer and Chaim on a
morning when one of the girls from Pinsk hanged herself in
the special compound he'd established for their comfort, "you
now see the results of taking too much time. They're flying
away from me. Get the numbers and nothing more. If you
make them say too much, they don't want to live. Stories don't
mean much in my reports."

Whatever punishment the colonel might have been about

to mete out to his translator — confining Leyzer Erlich to his
tent, forbidding the artist from wandering about with a
sketchpad, perhaps even kicking the wretched dog — all was
forgotten when Glibshin burst into the tent and said that if
the colonel was free, he should come outside and greet the
seventy-five children that the comrades from the Twenty-first
Infantry Regiment had just liberated from another camp.

"All Jews, Glibshin?"

"All."

The colonel threw up his hands and searched for a new
notepad. "Well, get the little man out there with them. Tell
him to do a few tricks, nothing more!" Poozie, you'll be relieved to learn, was thus spared the colonel's boot.

When Leyzer Erlich assisted the first little girl from the
truck, the dog performed faultlessly. "You want him to spin
a bit?" Leyzer asked. "You want to hear a story?" He checked
to see if the colonel was watching. "You have something to
tell me, *tsatskele*?"

Even though the magician was almost exactly her size, the
child, wrapped in a large blanket, grew rigid and fearful. She
shook her head and wiggled loose from Leyzer's hands and
pointed to the other children. For the first time since he'd
been with the Russians, Leyzer Erlich's soothing words and
kindly face (not to mention Poozie's strange contortions) took
second place to whatever was happening in one of the trucks.

"Come back here," Leyzer said in Yiddish, Polish, Russian,
and pidgin Magyar. "What is it?"

"Please, let me go up there," the girl said to a startled Leyzer
Erlich. "I want to sit by the man."

She ran over to the truck and was lifted onto the open cab
by a soldier.

"Let me see," the girl shouted. "I want to see what he's got."

Professional jealousy played its part in Leyzer's decision to pull himself above the truck's cab to see who'd usurped his official role as greeter and information-seeker. And when, after three attempts, he found a way to slide over and down the muddy windscreen, carefully balancing himself high enough so that he might exert his true authority, Leyzer Erlich, too, began to laugh (a bit louder, certainly with more strength) along with the seventy-five children who watched the blue-eyed Jew from Nowy Dwor turn a piece of cloth into a lion that roared and snapped.

"So the beast popped out of the jungle, crawled along to his house, and waited for nightfall. That night, the little Indian boy brought him a bowl of fruit and nuts and candies."

Here was our Chaim Turkow, voice intact enough to growl and roar, a little girl leaning over his shoulder as he crouched in the dirty truck. He'd even wrapped a colored cloth around is head. Aha, aha! And no one clapped louder than Leyzer Erlich when the tale was finished.

After a few more stories (some with monkeys, a few with whistling rabbits), Chaim Turkow led the children from the truck to where a soldier had begun cutting bread and pouring milk into tin cups. The children sat down without being asked. Chaim found the colonel and the dwarf inside the officer's tent.

"Yes, yes, you can stay with them," our colonel said, standing by a pile of ledgerbooks and forms. "But first, my notes: Names. Places. Events. I want to know who these children are."

The dwarf waved two small fingers in front of the colonel's chest. "They're twins without their brothers and sisters, Comrade Colonel," Leyzer said.

"Be specific," the officer told him. "I can't report anything without details."

It was difficult for the colonel to believe what the Jew was saying, despite everything he now knew.

"Write down what you just told me," said the colonel. "Do it in Russian. Be precise."

In a steady hand (another trick?), Leyzer Erlich wrote out a summary of what he'd often seen from the infirmary window in his own camp. "The doctors wanted to know," he wrote, paying careful attention to the curved Cyrillic letters, "if a twin's sibling shows outward pain when his brother or sister is thrown into the fire. Clerks watched the lucky ones and took notes. This happened to Jewish and Gypsy children. This is the way it was, I so swear. L. Erlich."

The colonel signed his name above Leyzer's brief paragraph. He could hear the Jew from Nowy Dwor entertaining the children. Their laughter came closer and closer to the officer's tent. It was Chaim Turkow who drew back the tent's flaps with a hand covered by a handkerchief lion. The children stood in a line, facing the officer.

"Go ahead, Hanna," the lion roared. "You're first."

"Hanna Silberstein, ten years old, from Wolpa."

"And you?"

"Uri Holster. I am eight and lived in Bobowa."

Each child followed the lead of the others — name, age, town — all except the seventy-fourth, a girl from Grodno who gave two names.

"Do you understand, Comrade Colonel? Is it clear?" Chaim Turkow asked.

✦   ✦   ✦

After four months, three days, and twelve hours — he'd calculated everything for his superiors — the colonel wired his official request to Lublin for a transfer. His reasons were, he noted, "well justified in light of my need to join victorious Soviet forces now entering Germany. Full documentation to follow by courier." But to his wife in Moscow, the colonel wrote a letter that caused the poor woman (she was a doctor serving in a military hospital) great anxiety as to his mental health, especially when her husband made several unintelligible statements about twins, a puppet, a dwarf who spoke Russian, and a performing dog with a wooden leg.

A few days later, while Leyzer Erlich was busy organizing baths for the twins and Chaim Turkow was searching throughout the compound for some paper to sketch on, the colonel sent for Captain Glibshin.

"You're in charge, Captain. From now on, you keep the records. Lublin says our work will be very important."

Glibshin was puzzled. "Work? Comrade Colonel — I don't understand."

"Lublin wants photographs for the trials. Evidence, Captain — when peace comes we can't hang Germans without proof for the world. Everything must be in order."

His bags already packed, the colonel joined his driver.

"But don't worry, Mikhail Leonivich — you can get plenty of help. Make the Jew from Nowy Dwor take the photos. He knows something about faces."

The colonel tapped his driver's shoulder. He pretended to doze as the car sped past the area where the dwarf directed the mass bathing. Leyzer was far too busy to wave, and Chaim Turkow couldn't take his eyes off the page on which he was sketching a freshly bathed Hanna Silberstein.

15

FROM A RICKETY BUNK inside his tent, Leyzer Erlich was often too tired to do anything but push aside the tent flaps and watch Chaim Turkow photographing the Jews. Beginning after first light each morning, scores of children and adults gathered in the area set aside for Chaim Turkow's camera. If the Jews Captain Glibshin sent to the Chaim were too unhealthy to sit up on the benches, a trick from Poozie attracted their vacant eyes to the camera. A promise of soup convinced Hasids with their heads and beards shorn, or former tailors and porters, dentists and farmers, to come and sit for the photographer who spoke to them so quietly.

The children, however, took more of Chaim's time, especially when they arrived at the compound in the last stages of starvation or typhus. Where eight, maybe nine healthy ones sat on the bench, sometimes up to fifteen sick ones (once, even twenty) crowded together. "It won't take me long," Chaim promised them. "Hold hands if you must."

Sometimes, if Leyzer saw the children becoming too restless or sullen, he forced himself from his cot and went to help Chaim. He washed his face and sucked a lozenge to stop his coughing so he could then try his best jokes or a few simple stories. However, most of the children never smiled and the magician soon knew he had failed in six languages and five Slavic dialects.

"Boopa, boopa, boo," Leyzer once said before a soldier saw him and told him to let the photographer do his work in peace, "watch the happy Poozie! Boopa, boopa, boo!"

✦ ✦ ✦

You must understand how a "boopa, boopa, boo" can hardly compete with a Polish or Serbian or Hungarian Jew blurting out, "Who comes from Grajevo? Low number 234431," or "Who has seen my brother, Leybel Golub from the Janowska camp? Leybel Golub, anyone? Locksmith Golub?"

The calls grew louder as more refugees were brought to the Soviet compound in trucks. "Mischa Greenberg came from Pinsk by way of Kiev. Do you know him?" "Aron or Sara Moskovitz, your brother wants you!"

Within a few weeks, wooden barracks with tin roofs replaced tents, and Glibshin's men no longer grumbled about poor food since the captain had arranged for "local contributions." Polish members of the Party strolled throughout the compound and promised to bring a New Poland from the ashes of the old (in fact, these former partisans brought nothing more than cases of vodka that tasted like bad potatoes). Some of the children from the camp's early days grew a bit fatter; a few died without crying.

At the end of a week when Glibshin was continuing to establish a good name for himself in Moscow by sending well-written documents and the Nowy Dwor Jew's excellent photographs to his superiors, Chaim Turkow wandered throughout the compound looking for anyone who might be from Nowy Dwor. Sometimes a Jew from another place, anxious to have an extra ration of bread or soup, would invent a meeting with someone from the town. "Yes, of course, I knew many people from that place," he'd say through a parched throat. "Tell me what she looked like again and then I can tell you what happened." Chaim listened to the story that quickly turned into a lie, nodded, and gave the Jew whatever food he had or could steal from the supply tent.

One late spring night, when Leyzer's coughing became louder, Chaim Turkow began working on a sketch of Leyzer. The magician dozed while Chaim drew. "It's over," someone shrieked before a volley of rifle shots began. "No more!" The dwarf bolted upright when a loud cheer broke out from the center of the darkened compound. Poozie, her fur up along her back, scurried from the tent and was soon lost in the crowd gathering around Captain Glibshin, who now rode on the shoulders of his men and fired two green and red flares into the evening air. A blaze of colored light followed the smell of magnesium and sulfur, and only then did the soldiers hear the dry handclapping of Jews from France, Slovakia, and most places in Poland, of at least a hundred survivors from the Hasidic courts in the Ukraine, and of three Italian Jews from Turin — for they also wanted to be heard at the moment Glibshin drunkenly announced the surrender of their mutual enemy.

"Comrades," Glibshin shouted under the light, "it's over at last!"

"Take me outside," Leyzer told Chaim. "I want to see everything."

The excitement, however, was too much for Poozie IV. In the middle of a spectacular leap through a wire hoop, her heart simply gave out. Bending over the dog's limp body, a Soviet private was doing his best to comfort Uri Holster and a few other children who were crying and carrying on.

"Have no fear, *Kinder*," Leyzer said with difficulty after he slowly made his way to the children. "Our Poozie has jumped all the way to the Blessed One."

Despite all of the excitement — the firing of flares, rifles, and one mortar shell that spewed billowing white smoke throughout the compound — Leyzer Erlich got Chaim's attention. The magician pointed to the late Poozie and the crying children. "Take the dog," he said when Chaim came close. "This is too much for the little ones. Walk slowly to the other side of the fence. I'll follow you."

Chaim Turkow picked up the dog and wound his way through the great celebration. The Russians were dancing with some of the Jewish women, while Glibshin, a hero to everyone, continued to shoot his flares. The Polish Party members waved a huge flag in front of a large fire.

Outside the compound fence, Chaim and Leyzer found a spot under a tree. The innkeeper's son dug a shallow grave for the small dog, and the magician fell to his knees and muttered a special prayer for her repose. "I can't walk anymore," Leyzer said when he was finished. "I can't do it. Here, take the fruit and make it look as if it came from me when we pass the children."

What, we ask you, could have been stranger than seeing the blond Jew carrying a dwarf past the dancing Russians and their officers? Or to see how the dwarf's body began to twitch and his eyes roll when a few of the children (they, after all, were worried, since they had never seen a man become so small in just a few weeks!) ran up to Chaim in time to see one almost-rotten banana appear from beneath Leyzer's hat? "Another one, please," Uri Holster begged. "Just one more."

"I'm not going to let you go back to your town by the Narew until you learn more about the Dutchman and the others,"

Leyzer said to Chaim after the children were given the rest of
Leyzer's fruit and a few sweet lozenges. "You think I'm going
into a hole before I'm ready?

"Boopa, boopa, boo!"

✦ ✦ ✦

By the next evening, the dwarf's eyes were beginning to cloud
over with a thin film, and he couldn't see the Russian soldiers
who danced and drank close to the open tent.

"A pen, some paper," Leyzer cried when Chaim placed him
on the cot facing the flaps. "Get the fountain pen and the best
paper you can find."

Chaim washed the dwarf's face. "Rest, Leyzer," he said.
"There will be time in the morning."

But Leyzer weakly pushed Chaim's hand away. More
coughing and wheezing in an out came before the dwarf had
enough air to whisper, "Write what I tell you. Don't miss a
word. I want that Jewish captain to have something for his
Moscow friends."

Chaim held the pen and Leyzer rested against the canvas
pillow.

"Put: 'To my Comrade, Captain Mikhail Leonivich Glibshin. I, Leyzer Erlich, offer you a grand salute for removing
me from our recent history.' "

Leyzer closed his eyes. He raised his hand and began scrib-
bling across the space in front of his face as if he, not Chaim,
were writing to the Russian Jew. Chaim heard many names
and the beginnings of a few stories.

When the magician's whispering became too soft to understand, Chaim lay next to him. Although he wasn't writing
what he heard, Chaim knew that he had to remember.

"Are you listening to me?" Leyzer asked. "Do you think the

Russian will understand about Zabno in '39 and how I was kept on a pink leash in the camp infirmary by a German officer? Give me your hand and I'll describe him."

Chaim nodded whenever Leyzer finished a story or part of a story. "Yes, of course, I've got it down, he lied. "Everything is on paper now."

By the time the compound was beginning to recover from the wild victory celebration — this happening around dawn — Chaim knew the names of almost every Jew the dwarf had memorized from the list a Kapo once gave him. "Hungarians, Chaim," he said with difficulty. "From a village close to Sarvar. So many of them — Arohnson, Hermann, was the first. He came a year after the Dutchman."

Somewhere past "Memelstein, Miriam," Chaim heard Captain Glibshin drunkenly begin to sing to his men. But the magician knew nothing of it because he was now panting with details — ages, the Hungarians' occupations, how the children huddled by their parents in the so-called Family Camp compound.

"Up, up," Leyzer said. "Lift me up so I can find it in my boot."

The dwarf let Chaim help him double over on the cot. He grabbed the heel of his worn boot, scraped away some glue, and pushed the heel to one side.

"This is what's left of the Hungarians," he said, holding up a thin sliver of bone. "Maybe it came from Miriam?"

Naturally, with all the noise made by so many ecstatic Russians and a few hundred Jews, no one heard Chaim Turkow singing to the dwarf, who continued to hold on to the sliver of bone even after his body grew cold. "Shu, sha," Chaim sang. "Papa . . . never . . . sleeps."

✦ ✦ ✦

We'll never know how Chaim Turkow did it: how he managed to bury the dwarf without anyone seeing him; how he
simply walked past a number of Soviet soldiers and returned
to the children's tent for Hanna Silberstein and Uri Holster
because they said they would never stay in the compound
without Chaim Turkow and his lion; how he managed to
obtain a Soviet field map of Poland from Glibshin's tent; how
he found a coin under a Polish peasant's cap to persuade him
to make a little more room in his cart for three very light Jews;
how he avoided having to show papers to anyone. The work
of a magician's student!

On the one road open for travel, the peasant's horse pulled
its load for about fifteen kilometers to a checkpoint supervised by the Russians. We can only close our eyes and imagine
what it looked like when Chaim Turkow, mindful of his position and lack of a transit pass in the line of Poles waiting to be
processed by a Russian soldier, began to dig his boot into a
pile of ripe horse manure when he was within five meters of
the checkpoint.

"Rub some of this over yourselves," he told the children,
"and don't say anything to the soldiers."

Chaim Turkow lifted the children to his shoulders. He
pushed ahead of a startled Polish family, and like Moses parting the Red Sea for some thirsty former pyramid-builders,
Chaim created a wide opening for himself and two children.

"This country is shit, the people smell like shit," an officer
was overheard saying when the bedraggled and pungent
beggar hobbled past him. "These three I don't want to touch.
Let them go!"

That night, cool and refreshing, was spent beside a haystack within earshot of a train's whistle. Chaim washed Hanna and Uri from a bottle of water he traded for another apple. He told them they were going to a town he knew well, and then Hanna let Uri rest with his head in her lap. When Uri began to cry because he couldn't stop thinking about Poozie, Chaim Turkow covered the children with his coat. "Come close to me," he said, bending a stick into the shape of a boat. And then he told his short, attentive companions the entire story of Noah (an interpretation remembered from a certain printer and writer), describing in great detail everything the old man saw vanish beneath the rising water that lapped at the sides of his magnificent ark — and only after Hanna fell asleep and began to snore against his shoulder did Chaim Turkow finally say Kaddish for the dwarf he still expected to see at any moment.

16

THE ASTUTE SOVIET cartographer who drew the lines measuring the precise distance between one Polish place and another would never have guessed that it could take Chaim Turkow and two children so long to travel five kilometers to a rail station. Actually, it was seven, since the map never took into account nonexistent roads, the hundred thousand refugees who made bridges impassable with their carts, wagons, and arguments, and the equal number of Red Army soldiers who soon gave up celebration of victory for the sake of nation-building.

But even seven kilometers covered by one former fool and two children should not, under the worst of circumstances, have taken more than one day at most, a bit longer if they had to find food or, God willing, a small container of fresh milk. Yet they had already been on the road for several days after Chaim finished Noah's story when almost all movement stopped, save that easy passage allowed the military vehicles and black sedans carrying Polish members of the Party to their new positions.

Chaim never allowed Hanna Silberstein and Uri Holster out of his sight. He begged permission from Russian soldiers to let them pass, offered bribes to policemen (even the promise of five apples didn't work!), bartered bread, cheese, or water from angry peasants, and found shelter under trees or caved-in barns — all this until the awful chaos was finally settled by some young Soviet officers whose faces had shown they were in no mood to make exceptions for a Polish Jew who now spoke passable Russian.

Despite Chaim's care, Uri Holster grew feverish during the third week of their trip, his forehead becoming so hot that Chaim sold his own pair of shoddy Russian boots for a liter of bad vodka, remembering how Elzbieta claimed an alcohol bath was the only way to keep a head from boiling over into "vapors." The boy's fever lasted for several days, and Uri began to yell for his twin brother in a language no one could understand.

"He'll die here," said one of the Poles who helped Chaim bathe the child. "Look at his eyes." Chaim Turkow, however, wouldn't let Uri go: he never left his side, he sang to him until his throat was raw, and maybe because he'd been without a voice for so long, he never stopped talking to both children. And suddenly, just as Uri's fever began to pass, Hanna — who was without fever *or* spots — wouldn't move any longer: her hands went limp, she began to stutter and hide her face behind the boy, sometimes whimpering from this malady without heat or color. Even some of the Russian soldiers shook their heads over the girl's condition, especially when her bowels gave way without warning.

On the morning when Hanna crawled next to Chaim and told him that the soldiers would probably come for her soon, Chaim, now the best student of several teachers, hugged the girl and said in a voice not completely his own (this, we are certain, was the dwarf's last and greatest trick), "It's time to come back to life and learn about the great Feliks Maximillian Walicki!"

"Who?" asked one of the Polish boys close to the Jews. "Walicki?"

"The Pole who built a model of the solar system in his bed-room and remade the world," Chaim answered, hoping that he could invent enough details to last until a road opened to the market square in Nowy Dwor.

We can skip the beginning of Chaim's story (it was intri-cate and filled with soothing introductory details about the Wawel Castle smells, cobbles, scores of priests, and the manner in which Polish women washed their clothes in the Vistula) that took an entire day to complete. But we should mention that several Polish children joined the Jews just as Chaim noted the kindness of Walicki's father ("a seller of peacock feathers and other colorful trinkets"). The Jews moved closer to one another; the Poles — three peasant boys who held hands and took off their caps — were wide-eyed and polite. Chaim switched languages for the sake of the Poles.

"And within Krakow," Chaim said, motioning for the Poles to come closer, "young Feliks came to love his Church and the priest who heard his confession every day, and he even liked to walk close to the Jews' synagogues in Kazimiersz. How-ever, with his agile mind, he grew bored with the repetition of prayers, holy incantations the Jesuits believed could ward off any illness or political disaster, and — pay attention, please! — with the explanation he received during his thirteenth year as to the real reason why, in the middle of a sunny afternoon in June, the moon crossed in front of the sun and blocked off the light from all of Krakow for at least thirty minutes!

" 'It's the devil's warning,' the priest told him. The citizens of Krakow suffered a terrible fear: men and women fainted in the streets, children ran under wagons only to be crushed by the wheels, and a host of stillbirths were later reported to the municipal authorities — all, you understand, because the moon shook hands with the sun in a perfectly natural way.

"Thus came to be," Chaim continued in the voice borrowed from Leyzer Erlich, "the beginning of Feliks Maximillian Walicki's dispute with all official explanations. He watched all of this transpire from his father's balcony, and was sick when he saw a child — not much older than our little Uri Holster — dragged away from under one of those wagons, his small head cleaved in two from the weight. 'Never again,' he promised himself. 'Never again should people be frightened of something that has a better explanation!' "

By the end of the second day, Hanna began to eat some bread soaked in milk, and Uri Holster never took his eyes off Chaim, except, of course to run to the bushes when his bladder became painful. The Poles now slept next to the Jewish children and the blond man with a cap who, though he knew the Jews' special language, couldn't, with such eyes, be one of *them*. Once, for an hour or two, a Soviet corporal who'd had a Polish grandmother eavesdropped and heard the Jew tell how Feliks Maximillian Walicki endured humiliation and defeat not long after he began to build an amazing apparatus in the attic of his suspicious father's house on Jana Street — where, because he made the most beautiful silver crucifixes for the Jesuits, he was allowed to borrow from the great Jagiellonian University library (on a June night, the anniversary of the eclipse) the five leather-bound notebooks of Mikolaj Kopernik.

"Such a discovery! The master's great secrets about the planetary motions were there — unguarded, dusty, and covered by flyspecks — and Walicki read every notebook, memorized the intricate and detailed drawings. 'I will show them how it works,' he yelled to his pillow. 'And then everything will be clear!' "

Chaim used a few crab apples and some stones to demonstrate how Walicki constructed the most beautiful replica of the solar system from purloined bits of metal and glass. Working at night for three years, said Chaim, shaping and casting the tiny orbs and wires, Walicki finished his first working model during the Lenten season. As Chaim spoke, one of the Polish boys began to twist some willow branches into the shapes detailed by the blond man; another rolled bits of stale bread into planetary balls.

Chaim continued. "What you need to know is this: all his work was for others. Feliks Maximillian Walicki himself knew Master Kopernik was correct. He also believed that God made everything. So why in the name of all the saints did Pan Feliks have to suffer and see it all come to nothing? Why, on the morning when he invited the distinguished faculty from the university to his father's house to see for themselves how it was the work of *God's nature* that made the moon pass in front of the sun — why was it that the black-frocked scholars and priests took one look at the contraption that shone from years of loving attention, threw their hands into their cassocks, and destroyed this mockery to the Lord? Was it fear? Superstition? An assault on the faith they'd learned since they were children in those cold seminaries in the countryside? All of this. Maybe more. Feliks introduced his machine as proof positive that Satan didn't exist and that there would never again be the need for a crushed child when the world went dark for ten minutes, but now his machine was snapped in two, shattered, and rested on the floor like that broken body beneath the wagon!"

The Poles wanted to cry when Chaim reached what *they* thought was the end of the story. Hanna Silberstein (she'd finally begun to move about soon after Walicki read the notebooks) and Uri Holster were lost in thought, trying to recover, we'd guess, the image of the planets that spun and buzzed in Walicki's room.

"And what did our believer Walicki do? He bowed to the angry priests and scholars. He begged their forgiveness with a promise that never, even if he lived to be as old as the city walls in Krakow, would he tamper with anything again. The Fathers were assured and left for a midmorning mass, and Walicki, finding his notes from the great Kopernik, read: 'It is enough that *my mind* understands. All of the magnificence of the Vistula came from a trickle somewhere. If they laugh, as they will, and if they accuse me of being crazed, I will start again until they understand. This *is* the order of things. *The order.*'"

Chaim stopped talking for a moment, then looked at Hanna Silberstein.

"Feliks Maximillian cut himself many times picking up the shards from his planets, but when he saw the last priest disappear into the shadows, he closed his attic shutters and immediately began to plan his next model — one with more perfectly shaped planets, a brighter sun, perhaps even colored glass.

"This new machine took two years to complete; it, too, was lost, when a violent thunderstorm started a fire that destroyed everything — his notes and drawings, the completed second model, some poetry. If he felt like throwing himself into the Vistula and thus taking the risk of being dumped into unconsecrated ground as a suicide, the feeling passed as soon as he remembered that he'd somehow forgotten to include one of the planets in his model. 'Move on, Walicki,' he murmured while he watched some fishermen drag out an enormous carp from the river, smack the fish over the head, and — this was the key to our scientist's resolve — give the dead creature to a little boy who, had he been alive when the darkness came during Walicki's childhood, would have fallen overboard in fear at the devil's presence."

"Away, devil," Uri Holster exclaimed when Chaim Turkow stopped speaking. "Find someone else!"

✦ ✦ ✦

A siren whined from the top of a car driven past all of the Poles by two Soviet officers. Orders were shouted in several languages. "The roads are open," they announced. "The trains are moving on new tracks . . . all thanks to the Red Army, comrades. Go home to your people!"

Chaim helped the children pack some bread and tinned fish into their sacks. The now-inseparable Uri and Hanna walked behind him while he shook hands with the Polish boys who wanted to know where this Walicki went after the fire. The Jew would say only that Walicki made seven models in all, "three more in Krakow — all lost at the hands of younger, less forgiving priests — and four more in the Tatra Mountains where, if you go to Zakopane, people will show you the one surviving model of Walicki's universe."

Blessings and farewells were exchanged, one of the Polish boys kissed Hanna three times and admired the low number tatooed on her slight forearm, comparing it with his own higher set of digits. The Russian corporal with the now-improved understanding of the Polish language gave Chaim

Turkow a pack of cigarettes and escorted the Jew and his children past the guards. "Come," he said as he helped them into a truck. "I'll drive you to the nearest rail station."

"Is there such a model left?" the corporal asked once they reached the crowded station. "Is this the truth?"

Chaim shouted his answer because he had to run and join the huge line of people waiting to board the next train. "Of course. Go to Zakopane on any day of the year and ask. People will bow and then, without laughing, will point to the sky and say, 'Walicki!'"

Sometime after this, when the train finally left, Chaim remembered at least a dozen songs his mother sang to her grandchildren (Uri fell asleep after he sang just two!). Hanna begged to be taught the fruit-under-the-coat trick she'd seen the dwarf perform a hundred times in the compound. When the girl started to practice quietly in front of the sleeping Uri Holster, Chaim tried to think of some other endings to Walicki's story because, as you know, a few good tricks are always useful during emergencies.

"Walicki!"

17

To those of you who've looked at some photographs of Polish cities turned into rubble and beige dust during the war years — the beautiful Warsaw, rival to Vienna, a huge mound of brick and open sewers; Lodz, her factories burned; Poznan like a body without a heart when the old town, built by eccentric Milanese architects, was swept away — this Poland would seem to be no better than a salted-over Carthage. A dead place, you might say. Hardly worth starting over again.

But if you'd come to Nowy Dwor by the river Narew with Chaim Turkow, Hanna Silberstein, and Uri Holster, you would have seen the market square filled with peasants and wagons, Polish children pointing at the Jewish girl holding a little boy's hand, a thriving trade in broken dishes and sickly chickens; and no doubt — at least on this day — you would have walked across the square where Mordcha Rostzat saw his twin sons beneath the bronze forelegs of the marshal's massive stallion.

Chaim Turkow sat down on the rim of the fountain, close to an old woman selling bags of goosefeathers from a cart.

"So soon," she said to him. "We never expected to see any of you come back."

Hanna Silberstein made Uri sit down next to Chaim. "Here," she said to the old woman, "is the son of innkeeper Turkow."

The woman dropped a sack of goosefeathers and inspected the flushed face of Chaim Turkow. She was almost nose-to-nose with the blond Jew.

When she was satisfied that a clear identification was possible despite her failing eyesight and the swirling goosefeather snow, she beckoned her fellow tradesmen to the fountain. She recalled once seeing this same Jew — "Small as a shrimp without a shell" — being led by his father to the Jew bathhouse. "I used to clean his father's kitchens," she said. "As Mary is my queen, I remember: this is the one who lost his wits in the steam!"

"Get on with you, Dorota, whoever saw one who looked like him?"

The old woman's abusive answer, the cackling of the peasants who joined ranks around the three Jews, Uri's whining, the sudden appearance of a militiaman — all made Chaim Turkow's homecoming a spectacle worth seeing. Commerce stopped and a few children began to tease Uri for hiding next to a girl. The fountain blew a mist over everyone close to the Jews. Feathers wafted down on Hanna and Uri. As had happened once before when some other Jews waited by this same fountain, a brown truck, tires squealing on the damp cobbles, made an impressive entrance from a side street — coming, in fact, from the corner where Jacob Schmul Milutsky's studio once stood as a symbol of art and culture and proof-taking — blowing warning blasts from its deafening horn.

Two men jumped from the truck and cleared a path for a third — a person of some importance who wore, despite the hot weather, a wool jacket and beret. Though he limped and completed each step with some pain, the official pushed into the crowd. He smiled at the Jews beside the piles of feathers and put his hand over his mouth when Chaim started to rise. When the crowd drew too close, to see what the official would say, he ordered his guards to bring these new people to the town hall. "I'll ride with them," he said. *"No incidents."*

Once the Jews were safely inside the car, the official said, in flawless Yiddish, to the Jew who caused commerce to stop, "At last, at last!"

It came as no surprise to the suspicious peasants who looked through the car's windows to see Party Magistrate Jerzy Fiatkowski embrace the blond Jew in the same way, one remarked, as he'd once held the bloated corpse of the Jew Milutsky. "You remember the one," an old woman said. "Milutsky — the old printer we pulled from the river just before the Jews left for good."

"Don't be frightened," Jerzy told Hanna and Uri as the car moved past the peasants. "We two learned to make pictures together. The best photographs and posters in Nowy Dwor!"

✦ ✦ ✦

It didn't take long for Party Magistrate Fiatkowski to learn all he needed to know about the lost years of Chaim Turkow. Jerzy had one of the women who cleaned his office look after Hanna and Uri in another room. "You're safe with me," he told the Jew. "Lublin has given me full power as the People's representative in the area."

Jerzy pushed aside a plate of ham and dark bread that someone had set next to his phone.

"I've learned to do without most things I'm entitled to," he whispered. Then, in Yiddish, he told Chaim Turkow what it was like to starve in the forests for so many years with a partisan unit. "We ate the bark and drank berry juice. Many died from wounds. Some froze. And when they caught one of us, they took ten times that many from the nearest village and shot them as well. We ran in circles, lived like animals until the Russians found us and taught us about the world. One day, I learned a simple truth from the Russians: Stalin had better guns than Polish partisans with no ideology. So I switched sides, and now those reactionary Home Army bastards want to try and make everything the way it was. My job is to find them and —" Jerzy stopped.

Chaim sat watching his old friend, waiting.

"I question them, find out where they've been hiding. Then, if I'm lucky, I give them over to better interrogators from Lublin." In the uncomfortable silence that followed, Jerzy turned away from Chaim.

"Show me what they did to my family," Chaim said in Polish. "I have to know."

Jerzy blocked the door. "I have a list of everyone who was taken away — what more do you need? A tour of the old Jewish quarter?"

Chaim nodded.

The magistrate pushed his chair closer to Chaim. "Sit. I'll pour drinks. It's too dark to see anything now."

It probably would have been better if Jerzy Fiatkowski had actually *said* something instead of drinking too much, his back propped against the door with his two guards waiting outside. For who was more qualified to describe what happened to Nowy Dwor's small ghetto than an excellent printer and occasional photographer who had also studied those Goya prints? Who indeed?

At last Chaim Turkow was given the list of names. Then, while the guards fell asleep in their chairs and Chaim Turkow read the smudged letters (all that was left of several generations of Turkows) over and over, Jerzy said, "Before I fled to the forest, I was on my cousin's roof when the Germans blew the whistles for the Jews to gather in the square."

When he finished talking, Nowy Dwor's most feared keeper of public order and socialist morality stumbled toward the door, his bad leg dragging behind him like a stick scratching the sand. "Well, if you still want to see . . ."

A trouserless guard appeared from the adjoining room when the magistrate stepped into the hallway. The dazed guard was told to sit down as the Jew, the one Comrade Fiatkowski actually hugged in the car, stepped around him.

Jerzy put his hand over the guard's revolver. "Let him go, Guzik — such things can be allowed at night."

Leaving the guard behind, Jerzy followed the Jew into the street. The full moon will help Turkow see, he thought — still, in memory of Jacob Schmul Milutsky, he cried in Yiddish, "Look for the sign on the corner, Chaim Turkow, the one that reads GATE TO PARADISE."

✦ ✦ ✦

Need we tell you that, a bit past the simple marker described by the magistrate, Chaim Turkow entered the ghetto? Is it necessary to explain how, on the first corner, the five members of bookseller Shtayn's family were no longer sleeping inside their shop? Or that, a few steps to the left of Shtayn's cracked window, master bootmaker Goldenbloom's shop (the boot-maker himself was mercifully childless, given the circum-stances that arose) was currently occupied by two Polish families who still hadn't saved enough zloty to repaint the

Yiddish sign? — NO MORE PAINFUL BLUNDERS WITH GOLDEN-BLOOM'S WALKING WONDERS.

"Go away," a woman shouted at Chaim from one of the upper stories. "There's nothing here for you."

Chaim kicked against bolted doors, he rattled windows. "Hanka Vaybohn! It's me, Moishe's son."

Somewhere between Feyglshtayn's shop and Manya Zucker's millinery for "young women of distinction" (another sign in need of repainting), Jerzy Fiatkowski caught up with the Jew who was causing such a disturbance. The new householders and shopkeepers of Nowy Dwor opened their windows and threw cans and rotten vegetables at the moonlit shadow. Poles stood on their balconies in nightshirts, some holding crying children. And one family, lately moved into the splendid house of lumber merchant Dovid Kahane, hung over the very balcony where Reb Kahane used to allow his two spinster daughters to stand on Sunday evenings ("Smile," Reb Kahane once ordered his daughters. "Many prospects cross in front of this house!").

The magistrate pointed menacingly at the hecklers. "Get inside with your families," he ordered. "Nothing's wrong here. Go to bed!"

A disembodied voice shot back through the darkness: "Screw you — Poland for the Poles!"

But windows shut as soon as people recognized the familiar beret and limping gait of Comrade Fiatkowski. "Go to bed, comrades," he repeated. "I know your names."

"And fuck you, Russian cocksucker," that same voice replied. "Oooh!"

Chaim kept pace with the strange rhythm of banging windows and curses. "Henrik Neftalin, I've come back," he cried with one bang. "Zofia Rybicka, where are you?"

He pounded at one door until a shutter flew open, and
before he could ask for a lost name, a man wearing a bloody
apron and holding a lamp leaned toward him. "Enough already!
How long will it take you to figure out that people —" A baby's
choked wailing made the man turn around. "Iwona," he
ordered from the doorway, "hit her on the rump. Use the
suction every minute."

Another lamp appeared at the door. A man pulled Chaim
into the hallway and told him to wait. "The doctor can't talk
to you now. A baby is coming, don't you see? Gorski's third."

"I want to find someone who —" Chaim shouted.

More crying, this time from Gorski's wife. The smell of
alcohol and rancid, sotted linen rushed out from a small bedroom where the woman lay on her side, curled around a midwife's hands. The doctor stood nearby, furious with the
incompetent midwife. "The rump, dammit. Pound the rump
and press her belly!"

Chaim stood in the bedroom doorway. "Where are they,
Pan Doctor?"

Before the doctor could wipe the cigarette ash from his lips,
Gorski the father switched on the electric lights. A dozen Poles
bounded into the bedroom and pushed aside the stranger who
was trying to talk to the doctor. "A salute to Marek Gorski's
new daughter!" they cheered.

The doctor, angry at the intrusion, came into the hallway.
He let the white light settle on Chaim's face, then grabbed the
Jew's arm. "Turkow? Moishe Turkow's son? You're the one
who got away in time?"

"Leave us alone," a woman next to the doctor mumbled.
"*We* live here now."

Magistrate Fiatkowski entered the house and found Chaim
Turkow surrounded by Poles.

"Tell him, Fiatkowski," said a husky voice. "Tell him the Jews can't have their houses back anymore. We suffered, too!"

"But he doesn't live *here*, Lidia," the doctor said through a heavy smoke cloud. "This is the Turkow son, from the inn, remember?"

The doctor couldn't avoid the many questions.

"By the river?"

"The Jew who had all those daughters?"

"Does he know?"

"Ask him if he knows, Pan Doctor. Go ahead," a woman said.

"How could the Jew be so stupid? Alina, give the doctor a drink."

Just as if he were announcing a slight birth complication, the doctor made Moishe Turkow's son take a chair. The Jew refused the offer of a cigarette.

"In seven hours," the doctor said slowly, "in December '42, the Jews went to the station with suitcases and families, got on the train, and left."

"They went south," a voice added. "Due south. It was cold that month."

The doctor put his hand on the Jew's shoulder. "And I swear to you, Chaim Turkow, there was nothing we could do to stop it."

There you have it! The end of several hundred years of piously observed sabbaths, discussions of Talmud and Cabbala, births and circumcisions, bathhouse ruminations, Purim carnivals, and a very active trade in clothing, books, and lumber, oohs and ahhs over those pictures of Palestine decorating the Zionist Hall, the Italian daughters of David Finkel, and the exuberant discussions hosted by Moishe Turkow in the front room of his spacious inn. All of the Jews, the physician said, went south.

There was enough respect for Moishe's son's grief to stop any further talking about the Jews. Chaim Turkow rose, leaned against the doctor, and almost fell, but it was the arrival of Uri Holster — crawling, we might add, through the legs of five people blocking his way to Chaim — that made the Poles begin to leave. The boy saluted, gave the new father an apple for his wife, and, as he'd never done before, took his friend Turkow outside for some fresh air.

"It wasn't our fault what happened," Gorski yelled after them. "None of this was our fault. We need a place to live."

Once outside, not far from the yet-to-be-removed sign, GATE TO PARADISE, Uri heard a deep grunting sound coming from behind him. The boy screamed and hid behind Chaim Turkow's legs. An old man smelling of riverbank mud and rank fish caught up with the Jews and removed his cap.

"Listen to me, Chaim Turkow, I was standing inside Gorski's place with you, so you'll please excuse me. But did your father ever tell you that it was me, Artur Makuch, who was there when he went swimming back and forth across the river in '22? Did he tell you how he scared the shit out of me when I saw him come swimming between bits of ice to where I was banging a carp on the head?

"It's just that you should know that I nearly fell into the water myself when he came churning over to me and I saw this Jew. So I said, 'What is it, friend? You tryin' to drown a good Christian?' Your father laughed, he was so happy, and he yelled, 'I've had a vision and I know what to do!' "

✦ ✦ ✦

A short while after Chaim's visit to the ghetto, Magistrate Fiatkowski arranged for Moishe Turkow's inn to be given over to his son. There were protests lodged by the six Polish families who'd settled into Moishe's comfortable rooms (now without most of the better furniture, since the pieces were hidden in the flats of several German widows in Hannover), but the magistrate's directive was law. Very official. Lublin had agreed.

"More Jews will be coming," he told Chaim. "They'll need quarters and food."

To atone for his silence about the ghetto, Jerzy also sent to the inn a number of things from Milutsky's studio: two boxes of art folios, one of sketches and paintings that Master Printer Milutsky had buried in his cellar shortly after Chaim Turkow left, a brown box filled with old photographs, a single notebook (the only one Jerzy found) with the original draft of Jacob's play for children, and, at the risk of political deviationism, the unframed portrait of Rosa Luxemburg.

"Keep the painting of Rosa in the old pantry," the magistrate told Chaim. "You can do what you want with the other stuff."

Later that same day, while Hanna, Uri, and a few of the magistrate's guards busied themselves cleaning Moishe's floors with disinfectant, Chaim Turkow sat alone on the stairway. He unwrapped a few of Milutsky's photographs, mostly faded, sepia-colored prints of weddings and Zionist demonstrations. When he found the folder that held Milutsky's play, Chaim slowly ran his hand over the chipped surface of the banister post where a Jewish innkeeper once let everyone in his house know how he, Moishe Turkow, now doubted God's mercy and wisdom.

18

I T WASN'T DIFFICULT for Chaim Turkow to see under the dim light of the dirty sliver of moon, since he'd been walking the streets of Nowy Dwor for weeks, often staying out until early morning before returning to the inn. At first, the Poles who came to recognize him thought the Jew was sure to lead them to the places where the former residents of Nowy Dwor had buried their gold, their silver candlesticks, and all their valuable watches or necklaces: so try to see Chaim Turkow, leather bag thrown over his shoulder, fingers black from pencils and charcoal, being followed by some Polish children sent by their parents to make sure the Yid wouldn't get away with anything. And then imagine the surprised look on a number of peasant faces when it was reported by nine-year-old Dariusz Kowoski that the dead innkeeper's son just poked through the old part of town and always "drew pictures of things he saw on the ground."

"Where does he go all day and night?" people asked.

"I swear by Mary," young Dariusz said, "he draws and doesn't dig up nothing."

"But what's he look at so hard?"

"Old things," the boy maintained. "Old things on the ground."

"But I heard those fifty-three Jews living at the inn are doing like kings with all their Bolshie clothes and Jesus only knows what else!" Dariusz's mother said. "So don't tell me he isn't up to something funny around the old Jew places."

Then there was a rush of hands at the boy by several people who knew in their hearts that he was hiding a pearl somewhere, certainly a banknote he found at the Jews' hiding place. "Old things, Mamushka," he cried before they pulled his jacket off. "He don't look at nothing else!"

✦ ✦ ✦

As Chaim Turkow was making sketch after sketch of anything that remained of the Jews of Nowy Dwor, several of the inn's healthier Jews wanted to leave Poland. Hersh Berl, who told the others that Poland was now little more than "bricks and shit," unpacked some of Milutsky's paintings of Jerusalem. "Look how many plum trees there are," Hersh said to the two Byelorussian Jews at the inn, who often sat by themselves. "This is the land we need to find."

While Hersh Berl held up one painting after another, Dr. Lewandowski — still loyal to his Jewish patients — was about to examine one of the skinnier children, a girl who often hid behind doors and refused to eat. The girl jumped when the doctor touched her stomach. "No, please," she yelled. "No!" Before the doctor could calm her with some soft talk, one of the Byelorussians jumped on the good doctor and sank his teeth into his shoulder.

"Get this bastard off me!" the doctor howled. "Help! Help!"

It took three men to pry the Jew from the doctor's neck: one to insert a stick between the doctor's lacerated skin and the Jew's teeth, two more to pull the Jew's fingers from around Dr.

Lewandowski's ears. Hersh Berl then yanked the Jew's head backward while Lyusha Blum scratched him and cursed.

"Pigs, Nazi pigs," the Byelorussian shrieked before he fell on the floor. "It will never stop!" His head now as bloody as Dr. Lewandowski's stained coat, the Byelorussian called out for his friend. "Don't let them touch her, Weiss. Stop them!"

Weiss stepped between the others and his friend, who spat a tooth on the floor. He spoke to the Byelorussian in their own language, nodding when he whispered a name.

"He won't hurt anyone, I promise," Weiss said to the others. "He was a doctor in Minsk, and he saw what happened to the children who had to go to the SS doctors in the camp. They made him help them, you see, because he had a reputation as an excellent surgeon."

Hersh Berl motioned for everyone, save Weiss and his friend, to leave the room. "Give them a little more time to learn that the war is over," he said, gesturing back toward the Byelorussians. "Because I know a place where all of us can live again."

"Even the biter who thinks he's been through such a bad time?" Lyusha Blum asked.

Hersh nodded.

"Better be careful about your predictions," Lyusha added, after checking to be sure the two crazies weren't listening. "Minsk has always had a bad reputation."

✦ ✦ ✦

Chaim Turkow, meanwhile, was trying to find his fruit in the shards of the old Jewish quarter, you see — for he thought there just wasn't anyone left to do the sketches of what was once a studyhouse filled with believers, or a corner of the market square where Lena Turkow once taught her daughters how to buy the fattest holiday chickens from the peasants. In all kinds of light, he thought, sitting on the floor in the deserted, filthy synagogue, in all kinds of light I can work.

Somehow, Jerzy Fiatkowski understood what the Jew was doing, having seen Chaim wandering around long after curfew. After all, Jerzy, too, had looked at the copies of Goya and he could still recite line after line of Yiddish poetry. "Leave the Jew to stare at his rubbish piles," he told his militiamen. "He has to learn how to finish his sentences."

The days passed too quickly for Chaim to do all he wished. He'd completed nearly seventy sketches — but that Polish boy was wrong about the angle of the Jew's vision: it wasn't directed groundward, toward some mysterious objects. ("Are they stones he keeps lookin' at?" the boy's mother persisted in asking. "Do they glitter?") He'd no interest in the way the synagogue's rafters had fallen over the holy ark or how the scattered, torn books were soaked through in the courtyard. What he was looking for — Dariusz's mother would surely have thought this idiocy at best — were the exact places where people once stood when they were jealous or guilty, piously mourning, or content with their warm clothes and beds; and what we've learned of these months Chaim Turkow spent in Nowy Dwor lets us believe that he never forgot anything. All this he knew:

Where the Hasids used to celebrate their weddings and where Reb Grobner's ugly son, Israel (a "toad of toads," the rabbi's wife once called the boy, "and just as slippery!"), was betrothed to Lyusha Blum's fifteen-year-old sister. And how some Polish teamsters stood outside the Blum house and sang patriotic songs because they wanted the Jews to know that they, too, could sing and dance just as well as anyone in Nowy Dwor (this was sketch eleven, complete with nervous father and groom peering outside at the Poles). In the stable once owned by Julius Grynberg (it was now a stable for militia cars), Chaim found the wood engraving Reb Grynberg carved above the stall of his favorite horse, River's Pride, depicting a religious Jew astride the horse, earlocks flying behind him as he chased a gremlin or short devil (sketch thirty-two: close attention paid to the stall carving, with a remembered Reb Grynberg standing beside his beautiful bay before the short devil turned the other way). And Chaim found the stool inside the bathhouse, the very one the hunchback always used to hoist himself into the hottest possible steam (sketch number forty).

"Cigarette?" Jerzy always asked when he found Chaim moving from one spot to another. "Have a smoke and relax a little before you fall into a ditch somewhere."

Jerzy always ordered his bodyguards to hide out of sight while he and the Jew sat in front of Milutsky's old shop. Sometimes Chaim would let his pencil wander haphazardly over a clean sheet of paper, but he usually tried to draw something recognizable: a shoe, the brass nameplate on Milutsky's splintered door, the magistrate's hand holding the decent American cigarette. "This is a Camel, friend," Jerzy said to Chaim. "Did you ever think we'd see a Camel in Nowy Dwor?"

Then, sometime after midnight on an evening when the priest was celebrating a special mass to commemorate the suffering of the many lost Polish patriots, Magistrate Fiatkowski told his friend that there were some in the town who really thought the Jews killed the Saviour and, since the return of a handful of Jews to the inn, maybe even something worse.

"Forgive me, Jerzy. There's something worse after everything that's happened?"

"Yeah, sure, artist: they think *you* and the other Jews brought the Party from over there where the sun comes up. We even have a new name for it: *Zydokommuna*! Good, eh? The Russians bleed all over the place for them and they still think you Jew-Bolshie types piss on the cross at night! What do you think Milutsky would have told them?"

Sketch sixty-nine was Magistrate Fiatkowski agreeing to stand where he once inked the press in Jacob Schmul Milutsky's printshop; Jerzy was amazed at how Chaim included Milutsky himself, hovering as he used to behind the backs of his best Polish assistant and — reason for more appreciation — also a likeness of the fourteen-year-old son of Moishe Turkow as he'd looked before he ever suspected he had to become a fool. "The first day I came here," Chaim said. "Do you remember?"

"Only one mistake, though, Reb Turkow — Jacob wore his cap like so," Jerzy said, and, without permission, did a bit of rubbing here and there on the paper. "He wore it like this, so you couldn't see his right ear at all. And he would have told you that now was the time to leave this country."

Chaim looked at the doctored sketch and agreed with the changes. Magistrate Fiatkowski lit another smoke, checked the position of his bodyguards, and nervously cupped a hand over the Jew's ear. He whispered (in Yiddish) that he wasn't taking town gossip lightly. "The Jews," he said, "have to leave the inn."

"Where should we vanish now?" Chaim asked, a bit too loud. "Where do you expect us to go this time?"

Jerzy tried the whispering again. "To that Palestine Hersh Berl and a few of the others talk about all the time with the women and the others. I'll be happy to help arrange passes and tickets, even if the British don't want any more sick Yids coming to upset the Arabs."

And for the offer of assistance, the magistrate asked to borrow Chaim's sketches for a little while. "I need to remember, too," he said, stuffing the papers into his briefcase.

Hiding behind a broken door some twenty meters away from the Party magistrate and the Jew, Dariusz Kowoski was certain, this time, that he saw the Jew hand something to the Red ass-kisser. "It must have been something valuable," the boy told his mother. "The Jew looked real worried."

✦ ✦ ✦

When he finally returned to the inn, Chaim climbed the stairs and rested on the shredded carpet that, in better times, was one of Moishe Turkow's prize possessions: a handwoven runner made, he told everyone, by Polish artisans from the mountains.

"Chaim, is that you?" asked Lyusha Blum from her room. "Did you see Hanna and the Byelorussian? Did they find you in town?"

Chaim shook his head. Lyusha told him about the biter from Minsk and how the girl had run off to tell Chaim that she had decided they all must go to Palestine.

"She fell in love with one of Milutsky's old paintings," the former seamstress said. "And Hersh hasn't stopped talking about what a wonderful place Palestine will be for children. We tried to stop her from leaving because it was getting dark, but Weiss, the other Byelorussian from Minsk, said that his friend would watch over the girl. 'He once had a family and four daughters,' Weiss told us. He said his friend would never let anything happen to another daughter again."

"How long ago?" Chaim asked.

"Two hours. And Uri Holster won't go to sleep until she gets back." Lyusha left Chaim on the stairs. "Hanna said you should look at Milutsky's paintings again," Lyusha said before she closed her door. "Especially if you've never seen plums and fig trees."

Chaim walked to his room, past the wing where the children slept.

"Psst, Reb Chaim," Uri Holster whispered through a crack in his door. "Quickly, you should come into our room!"

Beneath the cot, two of the youngest children were huddled with only their dirty feet exposed.

"Look at them" Uri said. "They won't come out because they say if we go to Palestine with Hersh Berl and Hanna, the Arab men will chase them with long swords. They spent all day listening to Hersh talk about how the Arabs like hot places and don't like Jews too much. I can't sleep with them crying under me!"

Chaim reached into the dark tunnel and felt a cold hand.

"Go away, you Arab," Nosm Litman moaned. "Ya, ya, ya!"

Uri Holster began to cry.

The Arab then crawled under the bed. Nosm Litman cowered when he saw the hand reaching out for him, and if Chaim Turkow hadn't remembered how the world was created by Jacob Schmul Milutsky, Nosm Litman (the only Litman to return to Nowy Dwor out of the eight who left) might have bitten the marauding Arab himself, or he would have forced Levi Dubner to attack, according to plan.

"Would you like to see the world made again, here in this room?" the artist asked over Uri's sniffling and sobs. "With a real sun, leaping fish, and maybe even the ocean with some waves?"

"You don't have a sword?" asked Levi Dubner.

"No sword. No Arab. Come out and see."

Nosm Litman and Levi Dubner emerged, arm in arm, from their Masada. Both boys had also been crying, and Chaim's charcoal-blackened hands didn't help alleviate any fears. Levi Dubner's face showed how disgusted he was by Uri's cowardice. "Baby," he yelled. "Feh!"

Chaim left their room and soon returned with Milutsky's play notebook and some of the printer's poems. Nosm, Levi, and a shamed Uri sat on the cot, waiting. Chaim found the sheaf of old papers beneath the husks of insects that marred the ribbon and the top pages. Chaim could still read the first act of "A Hopeful Beginning: Are First Things Always Good?" "People believe more of what you say when the lights pop off above them," Milutsky had scribbled on the top of the second page. "Always!"

Chaim soon had Levi Dubner playing a fish, Nosm content to be the new land, and Uri Holster, covered by a white sheet, playing a moving cloud. Marching around the room with a kerosene lantern, Chaim ordered the appearance of more and more living things: trees, elephants, lizards. Chaim soon threw off his heavenly veil and chased after the fish and the clouds. "Faster, faster," he said. "Don't stop."

When the loud knocking began, Uri Holster naturally thought that Chaim Turkow had decided to make some thunder. "Open up, please," a familiar voice said from the other side of the locked door.

The door handle and bolt were being pulled from the outside. The door gave way. "I'm sorry," Nosm immediately said in Polish when he saw the uniforms. "We were —"

The magistrate stepped in front of his senior militiamen and waved away some of the smoke they'd left in the hallway. "Come with me, Comrade Turkow, but make these boys stay inside."

A dozen Jews heard the commotion and gathered in the front hallway of the inn. Chaim Turkow followed Jerzy outside, to a cart that sagged under the weight of two fly-covered bundles.

"Listen, comrades, all of you!" said Magistrate Fiatkowski. "This is the work of fascist hooligans in this country." Then, when he nodded, the youngest officer pulled back the top portion of tarpaulin. "Hanna Silberstein," said the magistrate. "Eleven or twelve years." Another nod, another pulling back of a black cover. "And this," said the magistrate while trying to stand in front of the unrecognizable face and body, "must be one of the Byelorussians. The doctor can't figure out how old he was."

"Shush," someone on the porch said. "Shush!"

"The bodies were discovered by one Dorota Lukasek, near the main road, in a ravine," a young militiaman added. "There have, comrades, been several such incidents —"

Uri Holster, fighting the tight grip of Lyusha Blum, finally broke away and ran, the white sheet that was once a cloud trailing after him in the dirt. He reached the cart just as the magistrate's guards tried to prevent Chaim Turkow from lying down next to the girl in her greasy shroud. Uri stopped, found there was no room left for him, and instead, seeing a long stick by Jerzy's feet, chased a terrified mongrel toward the river Narew. "Go away," the boy was yelling after the frantic animal. "Ya, ya, ya!"

And Nosm Litman, though he was no longer afraid of any Arab, tried to squirm between the legs of several Jews so he could tell the magistrate that he would never speak a word of Polish again.

In all of the commotion, no one heard Weiss, the other Byelorussian, run into Moishe's inn and begin throwing himself against the parlor shelves that displayed the paintings and photographs of Nowy Dwor's late printer and engraver. "Kaffeblum," he shrieked in his Byelorussian accent, as he fell next to the printer's *Jerusalem at Dawn.* "His name was Henrik Kaffeblum!"

19

FIFTY-EIGHT MILES away from Tarnow, a group of Jews from Moishe Turkow's inn began to trade jokes and possessions with the two militiamen accompanying them to the Polish-Rumanian border. Of the original survivors, thirty-six Jews finally raised their hands when Hersh Berl asked, after Hanna Silberstein and Henrik Kaffeblum were buried, "Who among you still have enough strength for Jerusalem?" As for the rest: six ran away from the inn within a few hours, ten left by wagon for Germany and the easier life to be had in a French Displaced Persons camp, and one boy, Uri Holster, refused to leave the examining room of Dr. Lewandowski. "He can stay with me," the doctor told Chaim. "I promise to show him where the Jews used to live in town."

Carrying only a change of clothes, a parcel, and some charcoal pencils, Chaim Turkow sat behind a curtain in the last compartment with Levi Dubner and the Byelorussian. "It will be beautiful," Chaim told Levi. "They say that when the sun sets, the whole city lights up in reds and golds."

Weiss agreed with the late innkeeper's son. "You'll go to school," he told the boy, "learn how to speak like a real Hebrew scholar, and before you know it, you might even frighten a few Arabs yourself!"

Partly on the strength of these arguments, Levi Dubner lost some of the awful fear he'd had after the burials. But it was not so much the talk about Zion that made Levi keep his food down, or the tepid tea and fairy tales Lyusha Blum offered to him and Nosm Litman. Instead, it was Chaim Turkow who revived the boy's spirits by taking him to a baggage car at the far end of the slow train and — expert in the ways of partial recovery that he now was — pushed aside Levi's hair so the boy could see exactly how Leyzer Erlich performed some of his most astounding tricks.

"With one hand you make them think you're a know-nothing," Chaim told Levi. "You fuss with this, with that, and distract them from the real magic. It's a simple matter of moving their eyes away from what's really happening, nothing more."

"I can't do it."

"Try."

"I can't get my fingers around the apple."

"No one will notice that."

And so it went: from Tarnow to somewhere close to Krakow — where the train stalled, then broke down for want of a few hundred kilos of coal — Chaim Turkow instructed Levi Dubner. "Make people look at your eyes, not your hands," he said, remembering how the dwarf (it could have been his diminutive size) seemed to make every person he'd ever met stare into his brown eyes as if the answer to all problems lay within. "Twist a little bit, too . . . a bit of dancing never hurt a good magician."

Five or six hours must have passed before Hersh Berl finally noticed that Chaim and Levi were missing. Hersh searched every car until he found them in a pool of apple juice and hay.

The innkeeper's blond son, Berl saw, was showing the boy, who always looked as worried as an eighty-year-old man, some tricks and God knows what else. Both were laughing, and Levi had a little color in his sunken cheeks.

"Never do that again," Hersh yelled at Chaim.

"What?"

"Leave the rest of us for some stupid tricks."

"Hersh, please —"

"Never again, Chaim!"

Once the angry Hersh Berl left the baggage car (he mumbled "Fool" at Chaim's back), Levi begged a few more minutes of solitary practice.

"What did the man who invented this fruit trick look like?" the boy asked.

"He had beautiful hands and a jacket filled with surprises, and if —"

But before our Turkow could make the boy feel an even greater sense of wonder about the dwarf who'd once seen so much of the world (he considered telling an abbreviated version of the Walicki tale), Levi Dubner almost managed to make a brown wedge of apple appear in the artist's own pocket.

✦ ✦ ✦

The other Jews on the stalled train had food, clothing that was far too warm for the journey, some trinkets bartered from the peasant women who watched them leave the inn, and three dozen books from the ruined studyhouse in Nowy Dwor. The militiamen who accompanied them promised no harm would come to the "holidaymakers" as long as they were in People's Poland. But if there was any fear of more violence among these Jews, given the loss of Hanna Silberstein and the Byelorussian, it was understandable. Hersh had brought along two knives, and Lyusha Blum, who'd grown up among brothers, carried a bag of sharp stones.

"Just let them try and touch me," the seamstress said to the militiaman next to her. "They won't have any eyes left."

The militiaman, a boy with new fuzz on his cheeks, tried to smile. Instead of taking the stones away from the woman, he pointed to her wicker basket.

"These are beautiful blouses," he said to Lyusha. "How much will you take?"

"A two-story house with a shop on the bottom floor."

"No, I mean in cash."

"My mother's gold locket," the former seamstress replied, "the one that some good Polish neighbor dug up from our garden at home."

"I'm sorry, Pani . . ."

"Then give me seventy zloty in coin, comrade. I'm sure the locket will turn up someday!"

"Forty."

"Sold."

The trip continued without any problems. The happy militiamen were soon laden with all manner of prewar currency and other items that had no value in Palestine; most of the ardent Zionists avoided any talk of what they suspected the British would do if they caught another batch of lice-ridden Jews trying to sneak into the Holy Land; and Chaim Turkow spent every moment inside a cloud of cigarette smoke with Weiss from Minsk telling the Byelorussian (who said he used to be a librarian and wanted to know exactly how Chaim survived) everything about the Turkow family, Jacob Schmul Milutsky, and the years he'd spent with Herr Grunewald. The heavy smoking kept the other Jews away (not to mention the fear of Weiss the crazy Yid), and the former librarian who loved records and organization wrote everything down in a ledgerbook he'd taken from Moishe Turkow's pantry. He wrote and wrote while the Polish engineers searched for coal and water in the countryside — and if Weiss tired, Chaim talked and wrote at the same time. Levi Dubner sat beside Chaim and practiced a trick.

"Look what you're giving us," Hersh Berl overheard the Byelorussian telling Chaim when the sun grew whiter and hotter. Hersh strained to hear Turkow's reply, but the noise of so many Jews mumbling and shifting their packs from one place to another made the innkeeper's son's voice just another buzz without meaning. There was something about a girl, a time in the darkness, and many confused thoughts about pictures and photographs.

On the afternoon of the third day, the train stalled once again. It was a perfect time for Levi Dubner to leave Chaim and Weiss so he could show Nosm Litman his amazing trick.

"Close your eyes," the boy asked his friend. Nosm clamped both hands over his face, allowing just a bit of inspection to take place between his index and third fingers. He saw Levi hide the crab apple under his shirt and draw in as much air as he could. "Now you can look," Levi said, and before Nosm Litman laughed, Levi let out enough air to force the well-lubricated apple to slide upward and — here was the part Nosm couldn't understand — into Nosm's pocket.

"Do it again!" Nosm shouted. "Please." The same preparations resulted in another apple rolling out from beneath a sleeping militiaman's stained jacket — this, you understand, from a distance of two seats!

The commotion and tricks ceased when suddenly the train

backed over a coupling and began moving in the opposite direction via a little-used bridge. Reb Mahler fell against the compartment door where Chaim Turkow sat next to a busy Weiss. Hersh Berl stepped over the fallen baskets of fruit and bread. "Who's responsible for this?" he called up and down the adjacent carriage. "Why are we going the other way?" he shouted. "What's wrong?"

Lyusha Blum had already returned to the compartment with a Polish conductor who told the Jews and their militiamen about "a bit of trouble on the line."

"Fascists?" one of the militiamen asked, fingers closing around his Soviet rifle. "Trouble?"

Naturally, the conductor cringed when he saw the rifle make an upward sweep toward his head (it was a technique that had served the militiaman well when dealing with suspected collaborators).

"So where are we going then, brother worker?" the militiaman said.

"A bit north, then east to travel secure lines for a detour to the southwest. Ten, eleven hours at most."

The poor conductor nearly fainted from fear until Levi Dubner stepped in between the conductor and the militiaman. "Look in your pocket, sir," Levi said, laughing as he slid back to his place next to Nosm Litman. "You'll like it."

It's difficult to say which the conductor (or the militiaman) liked more: the three cherries he pulled oozing from his uniform pocket, or the laughter of the militiaman who, thanks be to the Polish saints, now stacked his rifle against a vacant seat.

"Wait until he takes off his hat," Levi whispered to Nosm Litman. "Just wait."

"Relax, holidaymakers," the soldier yelled over his shoulder.

"Militiaman Marek Gralik pledges his life to your safety." And then the guard and the conductor, who trusted each other's eyes, left the Jews.

"What can happen to a car full of Yid mumblers?" the conductor asked as they walked over the outstretched legs of Hersh Berl. "We should be grateful that they're finally leaving after all these years, friend!"

Without incident or further detours from this direction to that, the train made only five more unscheduled stops to pick up peasants. The devout Jews prayed and held discussions at the proper time, the men told the women to wash out their underclothes and clean up the messes made by the children too nervous to use the train's overflowing toilet. Hersh Berl unfolded his precious map of Palestine and, with the aid of a tiny electric torch, told those still interested that they could expect to be seasick on the blue area close to Haifa. Now everything was peaceful and uncomfortable; the hours passed; the children, including Nosm Litman, slept. And no one paid attention to Chaim Turkow and Weiss, the Byelorussian who'd acted so crazy in Moishe Turkow's pantry.

"*Where* did the pig bite you?" Weiss asked.

Chaim pointed to the exact spot on his leg.

"Ah," Weiss said.

"And then?" Weiss prodded. "Who found you?"

Chaim Turkow lowered his voice.

"Ah," the Byelorussian said a bit later. "*So you never knew!*"

"How could I?"

"And you couldn't push the sewer cover a little higher?"

No answer.

The librarian took off his glasses and blew a ring of smoke. He pointed at the wrapped parcel the magistrate had given

Chaim at the station. "At least you have something left. May I look at those sketches you made in Nowy Dowor?"

Chaim stroked Levi Dubner's back. The boy stirred only a little when Chaim pushed the parcel across the torn leather seat.

20

L EVI DUBNER later remembered having a nightmare filled with terrible images of Hanna Silberstein's body lying next to a ditch. In what seemed to be a film playing in his mind, Levi saw the faces of the men who'd thrown the girl from a moving automobile. In reel two — Levi would never forget how he saw all of this as if he were in a cinema hall in Poznan, waiting for an inept projectionist to find the proper reel — the scene switched to the puzzled expression of the peasant who found the girl under some pine boughs. "Why, she's a child," the peasant exclaimed before he heaved what was left of Hanna into a cart — but he didn't whip his horse until he first sampled the sweet juice he took from the little spring-driven compartment under the girl's coat. "Thank you, Jesus," he sighed. "Thank you."

Levi remembered everything that happened after he awoke from his dream and didn't know where he was, or: how he tried to stumble through the dark to where Chaim Turkow should have been sitting with Weiss; how black it was in the carriage without the lights when he slipped into Lyusha Blum's lap; how he kept seeing the peasant licking the succulent orange; how his bladder burned for so long. There was much snoring and shuffling of cramped legs, and no one heard the boy stumbling over bags and stacks of books. He even tripped over the young militiaman's feet.

"Get out of my way," the militiaman hissed. "Stand outside on the track if you need to piss. We ain't movin' now!"

It was only then, mind you, that Levi saw the lights from a small station shining on the militiaman's huge feet. "Go outside by the tracks and settle down," someone said. "There's a Jew who needs to sleep in here."

Levi climbed down the guardrail steps to the cinder platform. This was when, while painfully expelling the bad water he'd had for days, he saw the four dark figures arguing in Yiddish on a rail spur to his far left. Their voices — one was very angry, two were apologetic, and the fourth kept repeating, "But what else can I do?" — grew louder when the conductor yelled at them, "Five more minutes, you hear. Five!"

Levi buttoned his trousers. When he'd reached the last step into the carriage, he heard Chaim Turkow tell the other dark figures to get back on before they were left behind.

"And for what? What possible reason can you have?" Hersh Berl was shouting as he pulled at Chaim's coat. "For the sake of a few pictures you scratched out and lost? And now you want to walk through everything again? Who'll listen to you? Who's left?"

Creeping closer, Levi saw Chaim take some scraps of paper from the Byelorussian and throw them in front of Berl. "They're not right," he said. The train was blowing off huge puffs of black smoke, and Chaim's words were almost lost in the noise. "They've been changed."

"Chaim, come with me!" The boy's cry was loud enough to distract Chaim Turkow and to give Hersh and Avram Slotnick time to pull the innkeeper's son up onto the train. As the first blast from the whistle sounded from the engine, Levi Dubner ran to the torn-up sketches and scooped up as many scraps as he could before he, too, was pulled back onto the slowly moving train.

The train lurched forward. As suddenly as it started, the train stopped: one of the drunk militiamen began shooting into the darkness, perhaps at a wagon or a sickly cow. The Byelorussian who'd yanked Levi aboard held the boy and spoke in his ear. "You don't move anymore," he told Levi. "You don't get off trains anymore in Poland!"

"Look, it's Chaim," Levi shouted. "He's back outside, on the track —"

Weiss pushed the boy aside for a glimpse into the night. The moonlight gave enough illumination for him to know. Levi Dubner wanted to leap out the window to where Chaim Turkow was bent over a portion of track, sifting through some bits of wire, perhaps, or some papers.

"Ay" Levi screamed when he managed to wedge himself halfway out the window before Weiss caught him and held on. "Ay, Chaim, come back. What do you see there? Come and tell me!"

The shooting stopped and the train began to move — and still Moishe Turkow's son stooped next to the track. Finally, as the engine strained to pull its load to the south, he started to run with the train, quickly picking up enough speed to get close to Levi Dubner's window.

"Levi, Levi, Levi," Chaim said as he tossed the piece of wire through the window. "This is what he looked like. The one who taught me about the magic we do here."

The train moved faster, and Chaim Turkow couldn't keep up.

"He knew everything," Chaim shouted. "Everything!"

✦ ✦ ✦

Weiss held the boy. "Sit with me," he said, and then scooped him up without hearing any protest. Levi would never know whether what he heard that early morning from the librarian was part of his nightmare, another lost reel suddenly recovered in his head, or a part of the original show: Hanna's body in pine boughs, a sweet orange in her pocket, a grateful peasant with Christ's sweet gift running down his cheeks, and now this — "Levi, Levi, Levi" and holding a bent wire figure that looked something like a little man.

"Shh, listen," Weiss said as he shuffled through the larger scraps Levi held. "Do you recognize this face, or this one?"

The boy saw one Polish face after another: round faces with angular noses that had been turned into flat ones by some careful erasures and redrawing; and in one sketch, a family (there were several daughters) of Poles sitting on a spacious porch. " 'Workers enjoying a new day,' " Weiss read to the boy from the caption someone had written on the back of the sketch. " 'A new era begins!'

"You take a pencil, Levi. And if you know how to make a line change, or you know about inks and how they can be erased, you can change a Jewish nose into a Polish one. You want a family to be happy workers? A little change makes it possible. You want a book to lose its Hebrew letters and gain some Polish ones? Easy. Scratch here and that will do it. It seems our Magistrate Fiatkowski got ahold of Chaim's sketches. 'Let me use them for history,' he told our artist. 'No time for individual needs or singular losses anymore: no more Jews, just Poles and workers.' "

Levi started to cry — one can also do this in dreams — and the Byelorussian let the boy rest against his arm, next to the sketches a better magician than Leyzer Erlich had changed for the sake of the new history in Poland.

Later, unable to sleep, Levi Dubner watched the beginning of dawn slide into the carriage. As the sun rose, it threw a small shadow past by the wire figure on the boy's lap.

Levi thought he asked Weiss where Chaim Turkow would sleep that day, but he never heard the librarian say anything.

✦ ✦ ✦

Only Hersh Berl had seen Weiss light a candle and show the boy Levi some scraps of paper. But there was no time to listen to a boy babble on about what had happened to Chaim Turkow, since by morning the train was approaching the station at the Polish-Rumanian border. Here, the inn's Jews had to worry about showing their doubtful papers to Rumanian custom guards, offering thanks to Polish militiamen (who, as a courtesy, relieved the Jews of their now-useless zloty), and trying to explain the nature of their holiday to a very tired border guard.

But as they inched forward in the line to show their doctored transit papers, someone asked (we think it was Lyusha Blum), "Where is Chaim Turkow?"

Hersh Berl, nervous and hoarse, started to explain, but the Jews paid little attention to the ardent Zionist because a flustered guard who wanted all of this Jew-business to end began yelling at them. "Holidaymakers?" he asked in bad Polish. "Jewish holidaymakers?" The Hasids started to pray and Levi Dubner grew pale.

The line stopped. Lyusha Blum loosened her skirt and gave the guard a blouse she'd hidden under her clothing. "For your wife," she told him, and then, without embarrassment, she let the guard slip his hand under her skirt.

"Moment," he said to the Jews. "One moment for us here." Another guard smiled and stroked her leg, working his hand upward.

"So, Berl," Lyusha said when it was all over and one of the Rumanians was smiling. "You can tell me in the time it took this gentleman to find what he's looking for — Where is our artist, Chaim Turkow?"

And this is when the Jews learned about the previous night: about the sketches that were changed (a number where stolen) by a party magistrate eager to gain a foothold in the New Poland, which, like her savior to the east, didn't recognize national differences (noses and letters included!); about Chaim Turkow leaving the train; about Levi Dubner's nightmare. Hersh Berl struggled to find a way to explain why anyone would choose not to go to Palestine. Weiss lifted Levi Dubner high over the Rumanian's desk and planted the boy atop a stack of documents and Lyusha Blum's blouse.

Lyusha walked away from the Rumanian, who followed the seamstress to another platform while he absent-mindedly stamped the papers of the holidaymakers. "I love you," he kept shouting in his bad Polish to the seamstress once he was finally done with the other Jews. "Stay and wait with me. Another train comes later!"

"Crazy man Turkow," Hersh Berl said to Weiss and the boy, "goes back to the Polacks so they can beat him up or worse! He's more than an idiot — does he think the Poles will greet him as a long-lost kinsman with those blue eyes of his?"

"A fool," agreed Eliahu Kramer. "Absolutely!"

Hersh Berl wanted to hit the Byelorussian from Minsk. "You," he yelled. "It was you who talked Moishe's son into leaving! And for what, to risk never seeing Zion for the sake of staying here to doodle a few sketches of bones and dirt?"

The arguing continued while the Jews boarded a train the Rumanian guard directed them to, and, avoiding Hersh Berl, crowded around the librarian from Minsk — and it was here, in a hot, smoky carriage, during the sixteen hours it took the locomotive to pull them toward another border, that some of the Jews from Nowy Dwor listened to Weiss read, nonstop, from a ledger that contained a record of everything Chaim Turkow had told him.

"But why did he tell you?" Lyusha asked Weiss when the train was beyond Poland (and Chaim Turkow's story had passed through the snow trip to Modlin). "Why?"

Weiss smiled and adjusted his broken spectacles to fit the bridge of his nose. "Because, my beautiful seamstress, I never stopped believing that truth is possible to find before the next life."

"That's all?"

"No," said the librarian. "He also promised me that someday he'd go to Minsk!"

Shu. Sha.

21

DEAR READER: Many years later, long past the time when these events occurred, two Jews who had been at Moishe Turkow's inn — one a Byelorussian living in the room given to him by the kibbutz authorities, the other an importer of illustrated books for children living comfortably in Turin — would amend, correct, and occasionally argue about the original manuscript recopied from a Polish ledgerbook that, in the absence of their families, became a mutual passion and duty.

"What's the best way to start this?" came the question from Italy on a membrane-thin airletter after so much else had been written and discussed. The response from Israel was succinct.

"Let's begin with the map, shall we?"

Then, pleading for his friend to consider a fitting ending to what he called "a simple story," the librarian suggested they not forget to mention how Nosm Litman, standing on the open, slippery deck of an old garbage scow that was able to sneak past the entire British Royal Navy at the gates of Zion, managed, in front of at least two hundred thirty-eight Jews, to make an overripe banana pop out from the shirt of Hersh Berl.

After wishing his friend Levi Dubner well at the bottom of the letter, the Israeli attached a sketch recently arrived in

Jerusalem from the Soviet Union. In colored chalk, the sketch showed a blond, blue-eyed man next to a toothless old woman. "Two old Jews celebrate Passover in Minsk," the artist had written in indelible ink on the back. "Not far from the home of Henrik Kaffeblum."